SEVASTOPOL SKETCHES

(SEBASTOPOL SKETCHES)

By LEO TOLSTOY

Translated by LOUISE and AYLMER MAUDE

A Digireads.com Book
Digireads.com Publishing

Sevastopol Sketches (Sebastopol Sketches)
By Leo Tolstoy
Translated by Louis and Aylmer Maude
ISBN 10: 1-4209-4928-4
ISBN 13: 978-1-4209-4928-5

Please visit *www.digireads.com*

CONTENTS

SEVASTOPOL SKETCHES

acts like a guide
- Instruct, make
vivid

_sights, sounds, smells
-gleam then dark
-nature disrupted

5

SEVASTOPOL

IN DECEMBER 1854   *dark, gloomy*

The dawn has just begun to tinge the horizon above the Sapoún hill. The dark-blue surface of the sea has already thrown off the shadows of night, and lies waiting the appearance of the first sunbeam to sparkle merrily. A cold mist blows in from the bay; there is no snow—all is black—but the sharp morning frost creaks underfoot and makes the face tingle, while only the distant ceaseless murmur of the sea, now and then overpowered by the thunder of the cannons in Sevastopol, breaks the stillness of the morning. All is quiet on the ships. It strikes eight bells.

On the North Side the activity of day begins gradually to replace the stillness of night: here some soldiers, with clanking muskets, pass to relieve guard; here a doctor is already hurrying to the hospital; here a soldier has crept out of his dug-out, washed his bronzed face with icy water, and, turning towards the reddening east, is now praying, rapidly crossing himself; there a high and heavy cart, drawn by camels, passes with creaking wheels towards the cemetery, where the blood-stained corpses that load it almost to the top are to be buried. Approaching the harbour, you are struck by a peculiar smell of coal, dampness, and meat. Thousands of different things—firewood, meat, gabions, flour, iron, and so forth—are lying in heaps near the harbour. Soldiers of various regiments, with or without bags and muskets, crowd around, smoking, scolding, or helping to load the steamer which lies with smoking funnel close to the wharf. Boats filled with people of all sorts—soldiers, seamen, tradesmen and women—come and go.

"To the Gráfskaya?[1] here you are, your honour," and two or three old salts, getting out of their skiffs, offer their services.

You choose the nearest, step across the half-decayed carcass of a bay horse that lies in the mud beside the boat, and take your place at the rudder. The boat pulls off from the shore. Around you is the sea, now already glittering in the morning sun; before you, rowing steadily and silently, are the old sailor in a camel's hair coat, and a flaxen-haired boy. You look at the huge bulk of the striped ships, scattered far and near over the Roadstead; at the ships' boats, like black dots moving over the glittering azure; and, in another direction, at the handsome light-coloured buildings of the town, lit up by the rosy rays of the morning sun; and, again, at the frothy white outline of the breakwater, at the foam above the sunken ships, the ends of whose black masts sadly project here and there; at the enemy's fleet swaying on the crystal horizon of the sea, and at the salt bubbles dancing on the eddying wash made by the oars. You listen to the steady murmur of voices which reaches you across the water, and to the majestic sounds of the firing which, it seems to you, now grows stronger in Sevastopol.

Some feeling of courage or pride surely enters your soul, and the blood flows faster in your veins, at the thought that you, too, are in Sevastopol.

"Your honour, you're steering straight into the *Constantine*" says the old seaman, who has turned to see where you are steering.

---

[1] The landing-place here called the Gráfskaya, is evidently the one called the Ekateríninskaya on Todleben's plans of Sevastopol. The purpose of the map given in this volume being to elucidate the story, the Gráfskaya is shown where Tolstoy puts it, though no authority can be superior to Todleben's on such a matter.

"All her cannons are still on board,"[2] says the boy, examining the ship as he rows past her.

"Well, of course; she's a new ship. Kornílof himself lived on her," remarks the old seaman, also looking at her.

"Look where it has burst!" says the boy, after a long silence, watching a small white cloud of spreading smoke, which has suddenly appeared high above the South Bay, accompanied by the sharp report of an exploding bomb.

"That's *him* firing from the new battery to-day," adds the old man calmly, spitting on his hand. "Now then, pull away, Míshka, we'll get ahead of that longboat there." And your skiff travels faster over the broad swells of the Roadstead, really overtakes the heavy long-boat, laden with sacks and rowed by clumsy sailors who do not keep stroke, and—making its way among all sorts of boats moored there—reaches the Gráfskaya landing.

On the quay, soldiers in grey, sailors in black, and women in many colours throng noisily. Women are selling rolls, peasants with *samovárs*[3] are calling "hot *sbíten*,"[4] and here, on the very first steps, lie rusty cannon-balls, bombs, grape-shot, and cast-iron cannons of various calibres. A little beyond is a large open space where huge beams, gun-carriages, and sleeping soldiers are lying; horses, carts, green cannons, ammunition-waggons, and stacked muskets are standing; soldiers, sailors, officers, women, children, and dealers are moving about, and here and there a Cossack and an officer ride along, or a general drives by in a trap. To the right the street is blocked by a barricade with small cannon mounted in embrasures, and near them sits a sailor smoking away at his pipe. To the left is a handsome building with a date in Roman figures on the frontal, and near it stand soldiers with blood-stained stretchers—everywhere you see unpleasant indications of a war camp. Your first impressions are sure to be most unpleasant: the strange combination of camp and urban life, of a fine town and a dirty bivouac, is not only ugly, but looks like horrible disorder; it even seems to you that every one is frightened and in commotion, not knowing what to do. But look closer into the faces of these people moving about you, and you will come to quite a different conclusion. Take, for instance, this convoy soldier going to water those three bay horses and muttering something to himself, and doing it all so quietly that it is evident he will not lose himself in this motley crowd (which does not even exist for him), but will fulfill his duty, whatever it may be— watering a horse, or helping to drag cannon—as calmly, confidently, and with as much equanimity as if it were all happening in Toúla or Saransk. You will read the same in the face of that officer passing by in irreproachably white gloves; in the face of the sailor who sits smoking on the barricade; in the faces of the soldiers in the portico of what was once the Assembly Hall, and in the face of that young girl who, fearing to dirty her pink dress, jumps from stone to stone as she crosses the road.

Yes! disenchantment certainly awaits you if you are entering Sevastopol for the first time. You will look in vain, in any of the faces, for a trace of ardour, flurry, or even enthusiasm, determination, or readiness for death,—there is nothing of the kind. What you do see are every-day people, quietly occupied with their every-day business; so that perhaps you may reproach yourself for having felt undue enthusiasm, and may begin to doubt the justice of the ideas you had formed of the heroism of the defenders of

---

[2] Cannons were removed from the vessels for use on the fortifications.

[3] The *samovár*, or "self-boiler," is an urn in which water can be boiled and kept hot without any other fire having to be lit.

[4] A hot drink made with treacle and lemon, also sometimes with honey and spice.

Sevastopol, ideas founded on tales, descriptions, and the sights and sounds that reached you on the North Side of the Roadstead. But before giving way to such doubts, go to the bastions and see the defenders of Sevastopol where they are defending it; or, better still, go straight into that building opposite, formerly the Sevastopol Assembly Rooms, and in the portico of which the soldiers with stretchers are standing. There you will see the defenders of Sevastopol: you will see terrible, sad, solemn, and amusing, but astonishing and soul-elevating sights.

You enter the large Assembly Hall. At once, as soon as you open the door, the sight and smell of forty or fifty of the amputated and most severely wounded, some in beds but most on the floor, staggers you. Do not trust the feeling that detains you at the threshold; it is a bad feeling: go on; do not feel shame that you have come as if to *look at* the sufferers; do not hesitate to approach and speak to them. The unfortunate like to see a sympathetic human face, like to speak of their sufferings, and to hear words of love and pity. You pass between the rows of beds and look for some face less stern and full of suffering, that you can make up your mind to approach and speak to.

"Where are you wounded?" you hesitatingly and timidly ask an old and emaciated sailor, who, sitting up on his bed, is following you with kindly gaze as if inviting you to speak to him. I say "hesitatingly and timidly," because suffering seems to inspire not only deep pity and dread of offending the sufferer, but also deep respect.

"In my leg," replies the sailor, and you now notice by the way the folds of the blanket fall that he has lost one leg above the knee. "But the Lord be thanked," he adds, "I am now getting ready to leave the hospital."

"And is it long since you were wounded?"

"Well, it's over five weeks now, your honour."

"And are you still in pain?"

"No, I've no pain now; only when we have bad weather it feels as if the calf were aching, nothing else."

"And how did it happen that you were wounded?"

"It was at the Fifth Bastion, your honour, during the first bombardment. I trained the gun, and was just stepping across to the next embrasure, when *he* struck me in the leg. It was just as if I had stumbled into a hole, and I look—and the leg's gone!"

"Is it possible it did not hurt you then?"

"Nothing to speak of; it was only as if something hot had blown against my leg."

"Well, and afterwards?"

"And afterwards it was nothing much either, only it did smart when they drew the skin together. The chief thing, your honour, is not to think: if you don't think, it's nothing much. It mostly all comes of thinking."

At this moment a woman in a grey striped dress, with a black kerchief on her head, approaches you and joins in your conversation with the sailor. She begins to tell you about him: of his sufferings, the desperate condition he was in for four weeks; how, when he was wounded, he stopped his stretcher-bearers that he might see a volley from our battery; how the Grand-Dukes had spoken to him and given him twenty-five roubles, and he had told them he would like to return to the battery to teach the youngsters, if he could no longer work himself. As she says this all in a breath, the woman constantly looks from you to the sailor—who, with his face turned from her, is picking lint on his pillow—and her eyes are bright with some peculiar rapture.

"It's my missus, your honour!" remarks the sailor, with a look that seems to say, 'You must excuse her; it's a woman's way to say foolish things.'

You begin to understand the defenders of Sevastopol; without knowing why, you begin to feel ashamed of yourself before this man. To show your sympathy and admiration you are tempted to say too much; but the right words do not come, and you are dissatisfied with those that occur to you, so you bow down in silence before this quiet, unconscious greatness and firmness of spirit, that is ashamed to have its worth revealed.

"Well, God grant you a quick recovery," you say, and you stop in front of another patient, who, lying on the floor, seems to be awaiting death in unendurable agony.

This is a fair-haired man, with a pale and swollen face. He is lying on his back, with his left arm thrown back in a way that shows cruel suffering. He breathes hoarsely and with difficulty through his parched, open mouth; the leaden, blue eyes are turned upwards; the blanket has slipped, and from under it the bandaged remains of his right arm sticks out

The oppressive, corpse-like smell strikes you more strongly, and the devouring inner fever burning in all the sufferer's limbs seems to penetrate through you also.

"Is he unconscious?" you ask the woman, who has followed you and looks at you kindly as at a friend.

"No, he can still hear,—but he is very bad," she adds in a whisper. "I gave him some tea to-day—though he is a stranger one must have pity—and he could hardly drink it."

"How do you feel?" you ask him. The wounded man turns his eyes towards you, but neither sees you nor understands, and only says—

"My heart is on fire."

A little further on you see an old soldier changing his shirt His face and body are a kind of brick-red, and he is as gaunt as a skeleton. One arm is quite gone, taken right off at the socket. He is sitting up firmly, and has recovered; but you can see by the dull, dead look of his eyes, by the terrible gauntness of his body, and by the wrinkles on his face, that the best part of this man's life has been wasted by his sufferings.

On a bed on the other side you may see the pale, suffering, delicate face of a woman, her cheeks suffused with a feverish glow.

"That's the wife of one of our sailors,' says your guide. "She was hit in the leg by a bomb on the 5th;[5] she was taking her husband's dinner to him at the bastion."

"Have they amputated it?"

"Yes, above the knee."

Now, if your nerves are strong, go in at the door to the left; it is there they bandage and operate. There you will see doctors with pale, gloomy faces, and arms red with blood up to the elbows, busy by a bed on which lies a wounded man under chloroform. His eyes are open, and he utters, as if in delirium, incoherent, but sometimes simple and pathetic words. The doctors are engaged on the horrible but beneficent work of amputation. You will see the sharp, curved knife enter the healthy white flesh; you will see the wounded man come back to life with terrible heartrending screams and curses. You will see the doctor's assistant toss the amputated arm into a corner, and you will see, in the same room, another wounded man on a stretcher, watching the operation, and writhing and groaning, not so much with physical pain, as with the mental torture of anticipation. You will see ghastly sights that will rend your soul; you will see war, not with its orderly, beautiful, and brilliant ranks, its music and beating drums, its waving banners, its , generals on prancing horses, but war in its real aspect of blood, suffering, and death. . . .

---

[5] The first bombardment of Sevastopol took place on 5th October, old style, *i.e.* the 17th our style.

On coming out of this house of pain you will be sure to experience a sense of relief, you will take deeper breaths of the fresh air, and rejoice in the consciousness of your own health. But, at the same time, by the contemplation of these sufferings you will realise your own insignificance, and you will go to the bastions calmly and without hesitation. . .

"What matters the death and suffering of so insignificant a worm as I, compared to so many deaths, so much suffering? "But the sight of the clear sky, the brilliant sun, the beautiful town, the open church, and the soldiers moving in all directions, will soon bring your spirit back to its normal state of frivolity, its petty cares and absorption in the present. You may meet the funeral procession of an officer as it leaves the church, the pink coffin accompanied by waving banners and music, and the sound of firing from the bastions may reach your ears. But these things will not bring back your former thoughts. The funeral will seem a very beautiful military pageant; the sounds very beautiful warlike sounds; and neither to these sights nor to these sounds will you attach that clear and personal sense of suffering and death which came to you in the hospital.

Passing the church and the barricade, you enter that part of the town where the every-day life is most active. On both sides hang the signboards[6] of shops and restaurants. Tradesmen, women with bonnets or kerchiefs on their heads, dandified officers: all speaks of the firmness, self-confidence, and security of the inhabitants.

If you care to hear the conversation of army and navy officers enter the restaurant on the right There you are sure to hear talk about last night, about Fanny, about that affair of the 24th,[7] how dear and badly

"Things were confoundedly bad at our place today!" says, in a bass voice, a fair, beardless little naval officer with a green knitted scarf.

"Where's that?" asks another.

"Oh, in the Fourth Bastion," answers the young officer, and at the words "Fourth Bastion," you will certainly look more attentively, and even with some respect, at this fair-complexioned officer. The excessive freedom of his manner, his gesticulations, and his loud voice and laugh, which before had seemed to you impudent, now appear to indicate that peculiarly combative frame of mind noticeable in some young men after they have been in danger; but still you expect him to tell how bad it was in the Fourth Bastion because of the bombs and bullets. Not at all! it was bad because of the mud. "One can scarcely get to the battery," he continues, pointing to his boots, which are muddy even above the calves. "And I have lost my best gunner," says another, "hit right in the forehead." "Who's that? Mitúhin?" "No . . . but am I ever to have my veal? You rascal!" he adds, addressing the waiter. "Not Mitúhin but Abrámof—such a fine fellow! He was out in six sallies."

At another corner of the table, with plates of cutlets and peas before them, and a bottle of sour Crimean wine called "Bordeaux," sit two infantry officers. One of them, a young man with a red collar and two little stars on his cloak, is talking to the other, who has a black collar and no stars, about the Alma affair. The former has already been drinking, and by the pauses he makes, by the indecision in his face—expressing his doubt of being believed—and especially by the fact that his own part in the story is too important, and the affair is too dreadful, one sees that he is diverging considerably from the strict truth. But you do not care much for stories of this kind, which will long be

---

[6] Among a population largely illiterate, the signboards were usually pictorial. The bakers showed loaves and rolls, the bootmakers boots and shoes, &c. &c. served the cutlets are, and how such and such comrades have been killed.

[7] The 24th October, O. S. = 5th November N. S., i.e., the date of the battle of Inkerman.

current all over Russia; you want to get quickly to the bastions, especially to that Fourth Bastion about which you have been told so many and such different tales. When any one says, "I am going to the Fourth Bastion," a slight agitation or a too marked indifference is always noticeable in him; if men are joking they say, "You should be sent to the Fourth Bastion." When you meet some one carried on a stretcher, and ask, "Where from?" the answer usually is, "From the Fourth Bastion." Two quite different opinions are current concerning this terrible bastion:[8] that of those who have never been there, and who are convinced it is a certain grave for any one who goes there, and that of those who, like the fair-complexioned midshipman, live there, and who, when speaking of the Fourth Bastion, will tell you whether it is dry or muddy, and whether it is cold or warm in the dug-outs, and so forth.

During the half-hour you spent in the restaurant, the weather has changed. The mist that spread over the sea has gathered into dull, grey, moist clouds which hide the sun, and a kind of dismal sleet showers down and wets the roofs, the pavements, and the soldiers' overcoats.

Passing another barricade, you go through some doors to the right and up a broad street Beyond this barricade the houses on both sides of the street are unoccupied: there are no signboards, the doors are boarded up, the windows smashed; here a comer of the walls is knocked down, and there a roof is broken in. The buildings look like old veterans who have borne much sorrow and privation; they even seem to gaze proudly and somewhat contemptuously at you. On the road you stumble over cannon-balls that lie about, and into holes, full of water, made in the stony ground by bombs. You meet and overtake detachments of soldiers, Cossacks, officers, and occasionally a woman or a child-only it will not be a woman wearing a bonnet, but a sailor's wife wearing an old cloak and soldier's boots. Farther along the same street, after you have descended a little slope, you will notice that there are now no houses, but only ruined walls in strange heaps of bricks, boards, clay and beams, and before you, up a steep hill, you see a black, untidy space cut up by ditches. This space you are approaching is the Fourth Bastion. . . . Here you will meet still fewer people and no women at all, the soldiers walk briskly by, traces of blood may be seen on the road, and you are sure to meet four soldiers carrying a stretcher, and on the stretcher probably a pale, yellow face and a blood-stained overcoat. If you ask, " Where is he wounded?" the bearers, without looking at you, will answer crossly "in the leg" or "in the arm" if the man is not severely wounded; or they will remain sternly silent if no head is raised on the stretcher, and the man is either dead or badly wounded.

The whiz of cannon ball or bomb nearby, impresses you unpleasantly as you ascend the hill, and you at once understand the meaning of the sounds very differently from when they reached you in the town. Some peaceful and joyous memory will suddenly flash through your mind; consciousness of your own personality begins to supersede the activity of your observation: you are less attentive to all that is around you, and a disagreeable feeling of indecision suddenly seizes you. But, silencing this despicable little voice that has suddenly lifted itself within you at the sight of danger, you— especially after seeing a soldier run past you laughing, waving his arms, and slipping down the hill in the yellow mud—involuntarily expand your chest, raise your head higher, and clamber up the slippery clay hill. You have hardly gone a little way up, when bullets begin to whiz past you right and left, and you will, perhaps, consider whether you

---

[8] Called by the English the "Flagstaff Bastion,"

had not better walk inside the trench which runs parallel to the road; but the trench is full of such yellow, liquid, stinking mud, more than knee deep, that you are sure to choose the road, especially as *everybody* keeps to the road. After walking a couple of hundred yards, you come to a muddy place much cut up, surrounded by gabions, cellars, platforms, and dug-outs, and on which large cast-iron cannon are mounted and cannon balls lie piled in orderly heaps. All seems placed without any aim, connection, or order. Here a group of sailors are sitting in the battery; here, in the middle of the open space, half sunk in mud, lies a shattered cannon; and there a foot-soldier is crossing the battery, drawing his feet with difficulty out of the sticky mud. Everywhere, on all sides, and all about, you see bomb-fragments, unexploded bombs, cannon balls, and various traces of an encampment, all sunk in the liquid, sticky mud. You think you hear the thud of a cannon ball not far off, and you seem to hear the different sounds of bullets all around—some humming like bees, some whistling, and some rapidly flying past with a shrill screech—like the string of some instrument You hear the awful boom of a shot which sends a shock all through you, and seems most dreadful.

"So this is it, the Fourth Bastion! This is that terrible, truly dreadful spot!" So you think, experiencing a slight feeling of pride and a strong feeling of suppressed fear. But you are mistaken; this is, still, not the Fourth Bastion. This is only the Yazónovsky Redoubt—comparatively a very safe and not at all dreadful place. To get to the Fourth Bastion you must turn to the right, along that narrow trench, where a foot-soldier, stooping down, has just passed. In this trench you may again meet men with stretchers, and perhaps a sailor or a soldier with spades. You will see the mouths of mines, dug-outs into which only two men can crawl, and there you will see the Cossacks of the Black Sea Battalions, changing their boots, eating, smoking their pipes, and, in short, living. And you will see again the same stinking mud, the traces of camp life, and cast-iron refuse of every shape and form. When you have gone some three hundred steps more, you come out at another battery—a flat space with many holes, surrounded with gabions filled with earth, and cannons on platforms, and the whole walled in with earthworks. Here you will perhaps see four or five soldiers playing cards under shelter of the breastworks; and a naval officer, noticing that you are a stranger and inquisitive, is pleased to show you his 'household' and everything that can interest you. This officer, sitting on a cannon, rolls a yellow cigarette so composedly, walks from one embrasure to another so quietly, talks to you so calmly and without affectation, that, in spite of the bullets whizzing around you oftener than before, you yourself grow cooler, question him carefully, and listen to his stories. He will tell you (but only if you ask) about the bombardment on the 5th of October; will tell you how only one gun in his battery remained usable and only eight gunners were left of the whole crew, and how, all the same, next morning, the 6th, he fired all his guns. He will tell you how a bomb dropped into one of the dugouts and knocked over eleven sailors; he will show you from an embrasure the enemy's batteries and trenches, which are here not more than seventy-five to eighty-five yards distant. I am afraid, though, that when you lean out of the embrasure to have a look at the enemy, you will, under the influence of the whizzing bullets, not see anything; but if you do see anything, you will be much surprised to find that this whitish stone wall which is so near you, and from which puffs of white smoke keep bursting—that this white wall is the enemy: *he*, as the soldiers and sailors say.

It is even very likely that the naval officer, from vanity, or merely for a little recreation, will wish to show you some firing. "Call the gunner and crew to the cannon;" and fourteen sailors—clattering their hob-nailed boots on the platform, one putting his pipe in his pocket, another still chewing a rusk—quickly and cheerfully man the gun and begin loading. Look well into these faces, and note the bearing and carriage of these men. In every wrinkle, every muscle, in the breadth of these shoulders, the thickness of these legs in enormous boots: in every movement, quiet, firm, and deliberate, are seen the distinctive traits of that which forms the strength of the Russian—his simplicity and obstinacy.

Suddenly the most fearful roar strikes, not only your ears but your whole being, and makes you shudder all over. It is followed by the whistle of the receding ball, and a thick cloud of powder-smoke envelops you, the platform, and the moving black figures of the sailors. You will hear various comments by the sailors concerning this shot of ours, and you will notice their animation, the evidences of a feeling which you had not, perhaps, expected: the feeling' of animosity and thirst for vengeance which lies hidden in each man's soul. You will hear joyful exclamations: "It's gone right into the embrasure! It's killed two, I think . . . There, they're carrying them off!" "And now *hes* riled, and will send one this way," some one remarks; and really, soon after, you will see before you a flash and some smoke, the sentinel standing on the breastwork will call out "Ca-n-non," and then a ball will whiz past you and squash into the earth, throwing out a circle of stones and mud. The commander of the battery will be irritated by this shot, and will give orders to fire another and another cannon, the enemy will reply in like manner, and you will experience interesting sensations and see interesting sights. The sentinel will again call "Cannon!" and you will have the same sound and shock, and the mud will be splashed round as before. Or he will call out "Mortar!" and you will hear the regular and rather pleasant whistle—which it is difficult to connect with the thought of anything dreadful—of a bomb; you will hear this whistle coming nearer and faster towards you, then you will see a black ball, feel the shock as it strikes the ground, and will hear the ringing explosion. The bomb will fly apart into whizzing and shrieking fragments, stones will rattle into the air, and you will be bespattered with mud.

At these sounds you will experience a strange feeling of mingled pleasure and fear. At the moment you know the shot is flying towards you, you are sure to imagine that this shot will kill you, but a feeling of pride will support you, and no one will know of the knife that is cutting your heart But when the shot has flown past and has not hit you, you revive, and, though only for a moment, a glad, inexpressibly joyous feeling seizes you, so that you feel some peculiar delight in the danger—in this game of life and death—and wish that bombs and balls would fall nearer and nearer to you.

But again the sentinel, in his loud, thick voice, shouts "Mortar!" again a whistle, a fall, an explosion; and mingled with the last you are startled by the groans of a man. You approach the wounded man just as the stretchers are brought. Covered with blood and dirt he presents a strange, not human appearance. Part of the sailor's breast has been torn away. For the first few moments only terror, and the kind of feigned, premature look of suffering common to men in this state, are to be seen in his mud-besprinkled face; but when the stretcher is brought, and he himself lies down on it on his healthy side, you notice that his expression changes. His eyes shine more brightly, his teeth are clenched, with difficulty he raises his head higher, and when the stretcher is lifted he stops the bearers for a moment, and, turning to his comrades, says with an effort in a trembling voice, "Forgive me, brothers!"[9] He wishes to say more, something pathetic, but only

---

[9] "Forgive me" or "farewell" are almost interchangeable expressions in Russian. "Good-bye" (*prostcháyte*) etymologically means "forgive." The form (*prostíte*) here used, however, means primarily "forgive me."

repeats, "Forgive me, brothers!" At this moment a sailor approaches him, places the cap on the head the wounded man raises, and then quietly, placidly swinging his arms, returns to his cannon.

"That's the way with seven or eight every day," the naval officer remarks to you, answering the look of horror on your face, and he yawns as he rolls another yellow cigarette.

So now you have seen the defenders of Sevastopol where they are defending it, and, somehow, you return with a tranquil, heightened spirit, paying no heed to the balls and bombs whose whistle accompanies you all the way to the ruined theatre. The principal joyous thought you have brought away with you is a conviction of the strength of the Russian people; and this conviction you gained, not by looking at all those traverses, breastworks, cunningly interlacèd trenches, mines, cannon, one on top of the other, of which you could make nothing; but you have received it from the eyes, words, and actions—in short, from seeing what is called the "spirit"—of the defenders of Sevastopol. What they do is all done so simply, with so little effort, that you feel convinced they could do a hundred times as much. . . . You understand that the motive which actuates them is not that petty ambition or forgetfulness which you yourself experienced, but some stronger feeling, which has made of them beings who live quietly under the flying balls, facing a hundred chances of death instead of the one others are subjected to,—and this amid conditions of continual toil, lack of sleep, and dirt. For the sake of a cross, or promotion, or because of a threat, men could not accept such terrible conditions of life: there must be some other and higher motive power.

It is only now that the tales of the early days of the siege of Sevastopol are for you no longer beautiful historical legends, but have become realities: the tales of the time when it was not fortified, when there was no army to defend it, when it seemed a physical impossibility to retain it, and there was yet not the slightest idea of abandoning it to the enemy—of the time when Kornílof, that hero worthy of ancient Greece, making his round of the troops, said, "Lads, we will die, but we will not surrender Sevastopol!" and our Russians, incapable of phrase-making, replied, "We will die! Hurrah!" You will clearly recognise in the men you have just left the heroes whose spirits did not flag, but rose, during those dismal days, and who gladly prepared to die.

The evening closes in. The sun, just as it is setting, comes out from behind the grey clouds that covered the sky, and suddenly lights up with ruddy radiance the purple clouds, the greenish waters of the sea with ships and boats rocking on its broad even swell, the white buildings of the town, and the people moving along the streets. The sound of some old valse played by a military band on the boulevard is borne along the water, and seems, in some strange way, answered by the firing from the bastions.

Sevastopol, 25*th April*, o.s., 1855.

IN MAY 1855

I

dark, gloomy

Six months have passed since the first cannon ball whistled from the bastions of Sevastopol and threw up the earth of the enemy's entrenchments. Since then bullets, balls, and bombs by the thousand have been flying continually from the bastions to the entrenchments, and from the entrenchments to the bastions, and above them the angel of death has hovered unceasingly.

Thousands of human ambitions have had time to be wounded, thousands to be gratified and to expand, thousands to be lulled to rest in the arms of death. So many pink coffins and linen palls! And yet the same sounds from the bastions fill the air; still the French from their camp look with involuntary trepidation and fear at the yellowy earth of the bastions of Sevastopol, and count the embrasures from which the iron cannon frown fiercely; still the pilot from the elevation of the signal - station watches, as before, through the fixed telescope the bright-coloured figures of the French: their batteries, tents, their columns moving on the green hill, the puffs of smoke that rise from the entrenchments; and still, from many parts of the world, with the same ardour, crowds of different men, with still more different desires, stream to this fatal spot But the question the diplomatists have not settled still remains unsolved by powder and blood.

II

In the besieged town of Sevastopol a regimental band played on the boulevard near the pavilion, and crowds of women and military men strolled along the paths making holiday. The bright spring sun had risen in the morning above the English entrenchments, had reached the bastions, then the town, the Nicholas Barracks, shining with equal joy on all, and was now sinking towards the distant blue sea, which, rocking in even motion, glittered with silvery light.

A tall infantry officer with a slight stoop, drawing on a presentable though not very white glove, passed out of the gate of one of the small sailors' houses built on the left side of the Morskáya Street, and, gazing thoughtfully at the ground, ascended the hill towards the boulevard. The expression of his plain face did not reveal great intellectual power, but rather good-nature, common-sense, honesty, and an inclination towards respectability. He was badly built, and seemed a bit shy and awkward in his movements. He wore a nearly new cap, a thin cloak of a rather peculiar lilacky shade, from under which was visible a gold watch-chain, trousers with foot-straps, and clean, shiny calf-skin boots. He might have been a German (but that his features indicated his purely Russian origin), or an adjutant, or a regimental quartermaster (but in that case he would have had spurs), or an officer transferred for the campaign from the cavalry or the Guards. He was, in fact, an officer who had exchanged from the cavalry, and as he ascended the hill towards the boulevard, he was thinking of a letter he had received from a former comrade now retired from the army, a landed proprietor of the government of T——, and of his great friend, that comrade's wife, the pale, blue-eyed Natasha. He recalled one part of the letter, where his comrade wrote:—

"When we receive the *Invalide*,[10] Póupka" (so the retired Uhlan called his wife) "rushes headlong into the hall, seizes the paper, and runs with it to a seat in the *arbour* or the *drawing-room* (in which, you remember, we spent such jolly winter evenings when your regiment was stationed in our town), and reads of *your* heroic deeds with an ardour you cannot imagine. She often speaks of you. 'There now,' she says, 'Miháylof is a *darling*. I am ready to cover him with kisses when I see him. He *is fighting on the bastions*, and is certain to get a St George's Cross, and they'll write about him in the papers,' etc., etc., so that I am beginning to be quite jealous of you."

In another place he wrote: "The papers reach us awfully late, and though there are plenty of rumours, one cannot believe them all. For instance, those *young ladies with music* you know of were saying yesterday that Napoleon has been captured by our Cossacks and sent to St Petersburg; but you can guess how much of this I believe. One fresh arrival from Petersburg tells us for certain (he is sent by the Minister on special business, a capital fellow, and now there is no one in the town you can't think what a *resource* he is to us), that we have taken Eupatoria, *so that the French are cut off from Balaclava*, and that we lost 200 in the affair and the French as many as 15,000. The wife was in such raptures that she *caroused* all night, and said that a presentiment made her certain you have distinguished yourself in that affair."

In spite of the words and expressions I have purposely underlined, and the whole tone of the letter, Lieutenant-Captain Miháylof thought with an inexpressibly melancholy pleasure of his pale-faced provincial friend, and how in the evening he used to sit with her in the arbour talking *sentiment* He thought of his kind comrade the Uhlan; how the latter used to get angry and lose when they played cards in the study for kopéyka points, and how his wife used to laugh at him. He recalled the friendship these people had for him (perhaps he thought there was something more on the side of the pale-faced friend): these people and their surroundings flitted through his memory in a wonderfully sweet, joyously rosy light, and, smiling at the recollection, he put his hand to the pocket where this *dear* letter lay.

From these recollections Lieutenant-Captain Miháylof involuntarily passed to dreams and hopes. "How surprised and pleased Natasha will be," he thought as he passed along a narrow side-street, "when she reads in the *Invalide* of my being the first to climb on the cannon, and receiving the St George! I ought to be made full Captain on that former recommendation. Then I may easily become Major already this year by seniority, because so many of our fellows have been killed, and no doubt many more will be killed this campaign. Then there'll be more fighting, and I, as a well-known man, shall be entrusted with a regiment . . . then Lieutenant-Colonel, the order of St Anne . . . a Colonel" . . . and he was already a General, honouring with a visit Natasha, the widow of his comrade (who would be dead by that time according to the day-dream), when the sounds of the music on the boulevard reached his ears more distinctly, a crowd of people appeared before his eyes, and he awoke on the boulevard a Lieutenant-Captain of infantry as before.

---

[10] *The Army and Navy Gazette.*

III

He went first to the pavilion, near which was the band. Instead of music-stands, other soldiers of the same regiment were holding the music-books open before the players, and, looking on rather than listening, stood a circle of clerks, junkers,[11] and nursemaids with children. Most of the people who were standing, sitting, and sauntering round the pavilion were naval officers, adjutants, and white-gloved army officers. Along the broad avenue of the boulevard walked officers of all sorts and women of all sorts—a few of the latter in hats, but the greater part with kerchiefs on their heads (and some without either kerchiefs or hats)—but it was remarkable that there was not a single old woman amongst them—all were young. Lower down, in the scented alleys shaded by the white acacias, isolated groups sat or strolled.

No one was particularly glad to meet Lieutenant-Captain Miháylof on the boulevard, except, perhaps, Captain Obzhógof of his regiment, and Captain Soúslikof, who pressed his hand warmly; but the first of these wore camel's-hair trousers, no gloves, and a shabby overcoat, and his face was red and perspiring, and the second shouted so loud, and was so free and easy, that one felt ashamed to be seen walking with him, especially by those white-gloved officers (to one of them, an Adjutant, Miháylof bowed, and he might have bowed to another, a Staff-Officer whom he had twice met at the house of a mutual acquaintance). Besides, what was the fun of walking with Obzhógof and Soúslikof, when, as it was, he met them and shook hands with them six times a day? Was this what he had come to hear *the music* for?

He would have liked to accost the Adjutant whom he had bowed to, and to talk with those gentlemen; not at all that he wanted Captains Obzhógof and Soúslikof and Lieutenant Pashtétsky and others to see him talking to them, but simply because they were pleasant people, who knew all the news, and might have told him something.

But why is Lieutenant-Captain Miháylof afraid, and unable to muster courage to approach them? "And supposing they don't return my greeting," he thinks, "or merely bow and go on talking among themselves as if I were not there, or simply walk away and leave me standing among the *aristocrats?*" The word aristocrats (in the sense of the highest, select circle of any class) has lately gained great popularity in Russia, where one would think it ought not to exist. It has made its way to every part of the country and into every grade of society that is reached by vanity (and to what conditions of time and circumstance does this pitiful propensity not reach?). It is found among merchants, officials, clerks, officers,—in Sarátof, Mamadíshi, Vínnitza: wherever men are found. And since in the besieged town of Sevastopol there are many men, and consequently much vanity, the aristocrats are here also, though death hangs over each one, be he aristocrat or not.

To Captain Obzhógof, Lieutenant-Captain Miháylof was an aristocrat, and to Lieutenant-Captain Miháylof, Adjutant Kaloúgin was an aristocrat, because he was an adjutant and intimate with another adjutant. To Adjutant Kaloúgin, Count Nórdof was an aristocrat, because he was an aide-de-camp to the Emperor.

---

[11] The term junker, borrowed from the German and pronounced yunker, is used in Russian in more than one sense, but at the time of the Crimean war it meant a volunteer, usually of good family, who had not yet received a commission, but was not treated as a private, and on an emergency was allowed to take an officer's duty.

Vanity! vanity! vanity! everywhere, even on the brink of the grave and among men ready to die for a lofty cause. Vanity! It seems to be the characteristic feature and special malady of our time. How is it that among our predecessors no mention was made of this passion, as of small-pox and cholera? How is it that in our time there are only three kinds of people: those who, considering vanity an inevitably existing fact and therefore justifiable, freely submit to it; those who regard it as a sad but unavoidable condition; and those who act unconsciously and slavishly under its influence? Why did our Homers and Shakespeare speak of love, glory, and suffering, while the literature of to-day is an endless story of snobbery and vanity?

Twice the Lieutenant-Captain passed irresolutely by the group of *his aristocrats*, but drawing near them for the third time he made an effort and walked up to them. The group consisted of four officers: Adjutant Kaloúgin, Miháylof's acquaintance; Adjutant Prince Gáltsin, who was rather an aristocrat even for Kaloúgin himself; Lieutenant-Colonel Nefyórdof, one of the so-called "two hundred and twenty-two" society men (who, being on the retired list, re-entered the army for this war); and Cavalry Captain Praskoúhin, also of the "two hundred and twenty-two." Luckily for Miháylof, Kaloúgin was in splendid spirits (the General had just spoken to him in a very confidential manner, and Prince Gáltsin, who had arrived from Petersburg, was staying with him), so he did not think it beneath his dignity to shake hands with Miháylof, which was more than Praskoúhin did, though he had often met Miháylof on the bastion, had more than once drunk his wine and *vódka*, and even owed him twelve and a half roubles lost at cards. Not being yet well acquainted with Prince Gáltsin, he did not like to appear to be acquainted with a mere lieutenant-captain of infantry. So he only bowed slightly.

"Well, Captain," said Kaloúgin, "when will you be visiting the bastion again? Do you remember our meeting at the Schwartz Redoubt? Things were hot, weren't they, eh?"

"Yes, very," said Miháylof, and he remembered how, when making his way along the trench to the bastion, he had met Kaloúgin, walking along courageously, and smartly clanking his sabre.

"My turn's to-morrow by rights, but we have an officer ill," continued Miháylof, "so—"

He wanted to say that it was not his turn, but as the Commander of the 8th Company was ill, and only the Ensign was left in the company, he felt it his duty to offer to go in place of Lieutenant Nepshisétsky, and would therefore be at the bastion that evening. But Kaloúgin did not hear him out.

"I feel sure that something is going to happen in a day or two," he said to Prince Gáltsin.

"How about to-day? will nothing happen today?" Miháylof asked shyly, looking first at Kaloúgin and then at Gáltsin.

No one replied. Prince Gáltsin only puckered up his face in a curious way, and looking over Miháylof's cap, said, after a short silence—

"Fine girl that, with the red kerchief. Don't you know her, Captain?"

"She lives near my lodgings, she's a sailor's daughter," answered the Lieutenant-Captain.

"Come, let's have a good look at her."

And Prince Gáltsin gave one of his arms to Kaloúgin and the other to the Lieutenant-Captain, knowing he would thereby confer great pleasure on the latter, as was really the case.

The Lieutenant-Captain was superstitious, and considered it a great sin to amuse himself with women before going into action; but on this occasion he pretended to be a *roué*, which Prince Gáltsin and Kalóugin evidently did not believe, and which greatly surprised the girl with the red kerchief, who had more than once noticed how the Lieutenant - Captain blushed when he passed her window. Praskóuhin walked behind them, and kept touching Prince Gáltsin's arm and making various remarks in French; but as four people could not walk abreast on the path, he was obliged to go alone, until, on the second round, he took the arm of a well-known brave naval officer, Servyágin, who came up and spoke to him, being also anxious to join the aristocrats. And the well-known hero gladly passed his honest, muscular hand under the elbow of Praskóuhin, whom everybody, including especially Servyágin himself, knew to be a man no better than he should be. When (wishing to explain to Prince Gáltsin his acquaintance with this sailor) Praskóuhin whispered that this was the well-known hero, Prince Gáltsin, who had been on the Fourth Bastion the day before and had seen a shell burst at some twenty yards' distance, considering himself not less courageous than the newcomer and believing that many reputations are obtained by luck, paid not the slightest attention to Servyágin.

Lieutenant-Captain Miháylof found it so pleasant to walk in this company that he forgot his *dear* letter from T——, and his gloomy forebodings at the thought of having to go to the bastion. He remained with them till they began talking exclusively among themselves, avoiding his eyes to show that he might go, and at last walked away from him. But, all the same, the Lieutenant-Captain was contented, and when he passed Junker Baron Pesth, who was particularly conceited and self-satisfied since the previous night (when for the first time in his life he had been in the bomb-proof of the Fifth Bastion, and had consequently become a hero in his own estimation), he (the Captain) was not at all hurt by the suspiciously haughty expression with which the Junker saluted him.

IV

But hardly had the Lieutenant-Captain crossed the threshold of his lodgings, when very different thoughts entered his head. He saw his little room with its uneven earth floor, its crooked windows, the broken panes mended with paper, his old bedstead with two Toúla pistols and a rug (showing a lady on horseback) nailed to the wall above it,[12] as well as the dirty bed of the Junker who lived with him, with its cotton quilt. He saw his man, Nikita, with his rough, greasy hair, rise, scratching himself, from the floor; he saw his old cloak, his common boots, a little bundle tied in a handkerchief, prepared for him to take to the bastion, from which peeped a bit of cheese and the neck of a porter bottle containing *vódka*,—and he suddenly remembered that he had to' go with his company to spend the whole of the night at the lodgments.

"I shall certainly be killed to-night," thought the Lieutenant-Captain; "I feel I shall. And really there was no need for me to go,—I offered of my own accord. And it's always so: the one who offers himself always does get killed. And what is the matter with that confounded Nepshisétsky? He may not be ill at all; and they'll go and kill a man because of him—they certainly will. However, if they don't kill me I shall surely be recommended for promotion. I saw how pleased the Regimental Commander was when I said, 'Allow me to go if Lieutenant Nepshisétsky is ill' If I'm not made a Major, then I'll get the Order

---

[12] A common way in Russia of protecting a bed from the damp or cold of a wall is to nail a rug or carpet to the wall by the side of the bed.

of Vladimir for certain. Why, I am going to the bastion for the thirteenth time. Oh dear, the thirteenth! unlucky number! I am certain to be killed; I feel I shall; . . . but somebody had to go: the company can't go with only an Ensign. Supposing something was to happen. . . . Why, the honour of the regiment, the honour of the army is at stake. It is my *duty to* go. Yes, my sacred duty. . . . But I have a presentiment"

The Lieutenant-Captain forgot that it was not the first time he had felt this presentiment, that, in a greater or lesser degree, he had it whenever he was going to the bastion, and he did not know that, more or less strongly, every one has such forebodings before going into action. Having calmed himself by appealing to his sense of duty—which was highly developed in him and very strong—the Lieutenant-Captain sat down to the table and began writing a farewell letter to his father. Ten minutes later, having finished his letter, he rose from the table, his eyes wet with tears, and, repeating mentally all the prayers he knew, he began to dress. His rather tipsy and rude servant lazily handed him his new cloak (the old one, which the Lieutenant-Captain usually wore at the bastion, was not mended).

"Why is my cloak not mended? You do nothing but sleep," said Miháylof angrily.

"How sleep?" grumbled Nikíta; "one does nothing but run about like a dog the whole day—gets fagged, and mayn't even fall asleep!"

"I see you are again drunk."

"It's not on your money if I am, so you needn't scold me."

"Hold your tongue, blockhead!" shouted the Lieutenant-Captain, ready to strike the man.

Upset before, he was now quite out of patience and offended at the rudeness of Nikíta, whom he was fond of, and even spoilt, and who had lived with him for the last twelve years.

"Blockhead? blockhead?" repeated the servant. "And why do you, sir, abuse me and call me blockhead? You know what times these are? It is not right to scold."

Miháylof remembered where he was going, and felt ashamed.

"But you know, Nikíta, you would try any one's patience!" he said mildly. "That letter on the table to my father you may leave where it is; don't touch it," he added, reddening.

"Yes, sir," said Nikíta, becoming sentimental under the influence of the *vódka* he had drunk, as he said, on his own money, and blinking with an evident inclination to weep.

"But when, at the porch, the Lieutenant-Captain said "Good-bye, Nikíta," Nikíta burst into forced sobs and rushed to kiss his master's hand, saying "Good-bye, sir," in a broken voice. A sailor's widow who also stood at the porch could not, as a woman, help joining in this tender scene, and began wiping her eyes on her dirty sleeve, saying something about people who, though they were gentle-folks, took such sufferings upon themselves, while she, poor woman, was left a widow. And she told the tipsy Nikíta for the hundredth time about her sorrows; how her husband had been killed in the first *bandagement*, and how her hut had been shattered (the one she lived in now was not her own), and so on. After his master was gone, Nikíta lit his pipe, asked the landlady's little girl to go for some *vódka*, very soon left off crying, and even had a quarrel with the old woman about a pail which he said she had smashed.

"But perhaps I shall only be wounded," reasoned the Lieutenant-Captain with himself, arriving at the bastion with his company in the twilight. "But where? and how?—here or here?" he said to himself, mentally pointing to his chest and his stomach. "Supposing it were here" (he thought of his thighs) "and went right round? . . . But suppose it's here, and with a piece of a bomb, then it's all up."

The Lieutenant-Captain, passing along the trenches, safely reached the lodgments. It was in perfect darkness that he and a sapper-officer set the men to their work, after which he sat down in a hole under the breastwork. There was little firing; only now and again on our side or *his* there was a lightning flash, and the brilliant fuse of a bomb formed a fiery arc on the dark, star-speckled sky. But all the bombs fell far beyond or far to the right of the lodgment where the Lieutenant-Captain sat in his hole. He drank some *vódka*, ate some cheese, smoked a cigarette, prayed, and felt inclined for sleep.

V

Prince Gáltsin, Lieutenant-Colonel Nefyórdof, and Praskoúhin, whom no one had invited and with whom no one spoke, but who yet stuck to them, went to Kaloúgin's to tea.

"But you did not finish telling me about Váska Méndel," said Kaloúgin, when he had taken off his cloak, and sat in a soft easy-chair by the window unbuttoning the collar of his clean, starched shirt. "How did he get married?"

"It was a joke, my boy! . . . *Je vous dis, il y avait un temps, on ne parlait que de ça à Petersbourg,*"[13] said Prince Gáltsin, laughing, as he jumped up from the piano-stool, and sat down near Kaloúgin on the windowsill,[14] "a capital joke. I know all about it." . . . And he told, amusingly, cleverly, and with animation, some love story which we will omit, as it does not interest us.

It was noticeable that not only Prince Gáltsin but each of these gentlemen who established themselves, one on the window-sill, another with his legs in the air, and a third by the piano, seemed quite different people now to what they had been on the boulevard. There was none of the absurd arrogance and haughtiness which they had shown towards the infantry officers; here among themselves they were natural, and Kaloúgin and Prince Gáltsin in particular showed themselves very nice, merry, and good-natured young fellows. Their conversation was about their Petersburg fellow-officers and acquaintances. "What of Máslofsky?"

"Which one?—the Leib-Uhlan or the Horse Guard?"

"I know them both. The one in the Horse Guards I knew when he was a boy just out of school. But the eldest—is he a captain yet?"

"Oh yes, long ago."

"Is he still fussing about with his gipsy?"

"No, he has dropped her. . . ." And so on, in the same strain.

Later on Prince Gáltsin went to the piano, and sang a gipsy song capitally. Praskoúhin, chiming in, put in a second unasked, and did it so well that he was invited to continue, and this delighted him.

A servant brought tea, cream, and cracknels on a silver tray.

"Serve the Prince," said Kaloúgin.

"Is it not strange to think," said Gáltsin, taking his tea to the window, "that we're in a besieged town, and here's a *pi-aner-forty*, tea with cream, and a house such as I should really be glad to have in Petersburg?"

---

[13] "I tell you, at one time it was the only thing talked of in Petersburg."

[14] The thick walls of Russian houses allow ample space to sit or lounge by the windows.

"Why, if we had not even that," said the old, always dissatisfied Lieutenant-Colonel, "the continual uncertainty we are living in—seeing people killed day after day, and no end to it, would be intolerable. And to have dirt and discomfort added to it——"

"But our infantry officers," said Kaloúgin, "they live at the bastions with their men in the bomb-proofs, and eat soldiers' soup—what of them?"

"What of them? Well, though it's true they wear the same shirt for ten days at a time, they are heroes all the same—wonderful men."

Just then an infantry officer entered the room.

"I . . . I have orders . . . may I see the Gen . . . his Excellency? I have come with a message from General N.," he said, bowing shyly.

Kaloúgin rose, and, not returning the officer's bow, asked with an offensive, affected official smile if he would not have the goodness to wait; and without asking him to sit down or taking any further notice of him, turned to Gáltsin and began talking French, so that the poor officer, left alone in the middle of the room, did not in the least know what to do with himself.

"It is a matter of the utmost urgency, sir," said the officer, after a short silence.

"Ah! well, then, come if you please," said Kaloúgin, putting on his cloak, and accompanying the officer to the door.

* * * * *

"Eh bien, messieurs, je crois, que cela chauffera cette nuit,"[15] said Kaloúgin, when he returned from the General's.

"Ah! what is it?—a sortie?" asked the others.

"That I don't know; you will see for yourselves," replied Kaloúgin, with a mysterious smile.

"And my commander is at the bastion, so I suppose I must go too," said Praskoúhin, buckling on his sabre.

No one replied; it was his business to know whether he had to go or not.

Praskoúhin and Nefyórdof left, to go to their appointed posts.

"Good-bye, gentlemen. *Au revoir!* We'll meet again before the night is over," shouted Kaloúgin from the window, as Praskoúhin and Nefyórdof, stooping in their Cossack saddles, trotted past. The tramp of their Cossack horses soon died away in the dark street.

"Non, dites moi, est-ce qu'il y aura véritablement quelque chose cette nuit,"[16] said Gáltsin, as he lounged in the window-sill beside Kaloúgin, and watched the bombs that rose above the bastions.

"I can tell *you*, you see . . . you have been to the bastions? (Gáltsin nodded, though he had only once been to the Fourth Bastion.) You remember just in front of our lunette there is a trench," . . . and Kaloúgin, with the air of one who without being a specialist considers his military judgment very sound, began somewhat confusedly, and misusing the technical terms, to explain the position of the enemy and of our own works, and the plan of the intended action.

"But, I say, they're banging away at the lodgments. Oho! I wonder if that is ours or *his?* . . . Now it's burst," said they, as they lounged on the window-sill looking at the fiery

---

[15] "Well, gentlemen, I think there will be warm work tonight."
[16] "No, tell me, will there really be anything on to-night?"

trails of the bombs crossing one another in the air, at flashes that for a moment lit up the dark sky, at the puffs of white smoke, and listened to the more and more frequent reports of the firing.

"*Quel charmant coup d'œil! a?*"[17] said Kaloúgin, drawing his guest's attention to the really beautiful sight "Do you know, you sometimes can't distinguish a bomb from a star."

"Yes, I thought that was a star just now, and then saw it fall . . there! it's burst. And that big star—what do you call it?—looks just like a bomb."

"Do you know, I am so used to these bombs that I am sure when I'm back in Russia, I shall think I see bombs every starlight night—one gets so used to them."

"But had not I better join this sortie?" said Prince Gáltsin, after a moment's pause.

"Humbug! my dear fellow! don't think of such a thing! Besides, I won't let you," answered Kaloúgin. "You will have plenty of opportunities later on!"

"Really? You think I need not go, eh?"

At that moment, from the direction in which these gentlemen were looking, amid the boom of the cannon came the terrible rattle of musketry, and thousands of little fires, flaming up in quick succession, flashed all along the line.

"There! now it's the real thing!" said Kaloúgin. "I can't keep cool when I hear the noise of muskets; it seems, you know, to seize one's very soul. There's an *hurrah!*" he added, listening intently to the distant and prolonged roar of hundreds of voices," Ah—ah—ah," which came from the bastions.

"Whose *hurrah* was it? there's or ours?"

"I don't know, but it's hand-to-hand fighting now, for the firing has ceased."

At that moment an officer, followed by a Cossack, galloped under the window and alighted from his horse at the porch.

"Where from?"

"From the bastion. I want the General."

"Come along. Well, what's happened?"

"The lodgments have been attacked—and occupied—the French brought up tremendous reserves—attacked us—we had only two battalions," said the officer, panting. He was the same officer who had been there that evening, but though he was now out of breath, he walked with full self-possession to the door.

"Well, have we retreated?" asked Kaloúgin.

"No," angrily replied the officer; "another battalion came up in time—we drove them back, but the Colonel is killed and many officers. I have orders to ask for reinforcements."

And, saying this, he went with Kaloúgin to the General's, where we shall not follow him.

Five minutes later Kaloúgin was already on his Cossack horse (again in the semi-Cossack manner which I have noticed that all Adjutants, for some reason, seem to consider the proper thing), and rode off at a trot towards the bastion to deliver some orders, and await the final result of the affair. Prince Gáltsin, under the influence of that oppressive excitement usually produced in a spectator by proximity to an action in which he is not engaged, went out and began aimlessly pacing up and down the street.

---

[17] "What a charming sight! eh?"

VI

Soldiers passed carrying the wounded on stretchers or leading them under their arms. It was quite dark in the streets; only here and there one saw lights, in the hospital windows or where some officers were sitting up. From the bastions still came the thunder of cannon and the rattle of muskets,[18] and the lights continued to flash in the dark sky as before. From time to time you heard trampling hoofs as an orderly galloped past, or the groans of a wounded man, the steps and voices of stretcher-bearers, or the words of some frightened women who had come out into their porches to watch the cannonade.

Among the spectators were our friend Nikita, the old sailor's widow, with whom he had again made friends, and her ten-year-old daughter.

"O Lord God! Holy Mary, Mother of God!" said the old woman, sighing, as she looked at the bombs that kept flying across from side to side like balls of fire: "what horrors! what horrors! Ah, ah! oh, oh! Even at the first *bandagement* it wasn't like that. Look now, where the cursed thing has burst, just over our house in the suburb."

"No, that's further, they keep tumbling into Aunt Irena's garden," said the girl.

"And where, where is master now?" drawled Nikita, who was not quite sober yet. "Oh! how I love that 'ere master of mine even I myself don't know. I love him so that, should he be killed in a sinful way, which God forbid, then, would you believe it, granny, after that I myself don't know what I wouldn't do to myself! S'elp me, I don't! . . . My master is that sort, there's only one word for it. Could one change him for such as them there, playing cards? What are they? Ugh! there's only one word for it!" concluded Nikita, pointing to the lighted window of his master's room, to which, in the absence of the Lieutenant-Captain, the Junker Zhvadchévsky had invited Sub-Lieutenants Ougróvich and Nepshisétsky (whose face was swollen), and was having a spree in honour of a medal he had received.

"Look at the stars, look at 'em, how they're rolling!" The little girl broke the silence that followed Nikita's words. She stood gazing at the sky. "Here's another rolled down. What is it a sign of, eh, mother?"

"They'll smash up our hut altogether," said the old woman with a sigh, leaving her daughter unanswered.

"As we went there to-day with uncle, mother," continued, in a sing-song tone, the little girl, who had become talkative, "there was such a b—i—g cannon ball inside the room, close to the cupboard. *A'spose* it had smashed in through the passage, and right into the room, such a big one—you couldn't lift it."

"Those who had husbands and money all moved away," said the old woman, "and there's the hut, all that was left me, and that's been smashed. Just look at *him* blazing away! The fiend! . . . O Lord, O Lord!"

"And just as we were going out, comes a bomb fly—ing, and goes and bur—sts and co—o—vers us with dust. A bit of it nearly hit me and uncle."

---

[18] Rifles, except some clumsy *stutzers*, had not been introduced into the Russian army, but were used by the besiegers, who had a yet greater advantage in their artillery. It is characteristic of Tolstoy that, occupied with men rather than mechanics, he does rot, in these Sketches, dwell on this disparity of weapons.

VII

More and more wounded, carried on stretchers, or walking supported by others and talking loudly, passed Prince Gáltsin.

"Up they sprang, friends," said the bass voice of a tall soldier, carrying two guns over his shoulder, "up they sprang, shouting' Allah! Allah!"[19] and just climbing one over another. You kill one, and another's there, you couldn't do anything; no end of 'em——"

But at this point in the story Gáltsin interrupted him.

"You are from the bastion?"

"Just so, y'r honour!"

"Well, what happened, tell me?"

"What happened? Well, y'r honour, such a force of 'em poured down on us over the rampart, it was all up. They quite overpowered us, y'r honour!"

"Overpowered? . . . but you repulsed them?"

"How's one to repulse 'em, when *his* whole force came on, killed all our men, and no re'forcements are given?"

The soldier was mistaken, the trench remained ours; but it is a curious fact, which any one may notice, that a soldier wounded in action always thinks the affair lost, and imagines it to have been a very bloody fight.

"How is that? I was told they had been repulsed," said Gáltsin irritably. "Perhaps they were driven back after you left? Is it long since you came away?"

"I am straight from there, y'r honour!" answered the soldier; "it is hardly possible; they must have kept the trench, *he* overpowered us quite."

"How are you not ashamed to have lost the trench? It's awful!" said Gáltsin, provoked at such indifference.

"What if *he'd* the force?" muttered the soldier.

"Ah, y'r honour," began a soldier from a stretcher which had just come up to them, "how could we help giving it up when *he* had killed almost all our men? If we had the force we wouldn't have given it up, not for nothing. But as it was what could one do? I stuck one, and then something hits me. Oh, oh—h! steady, lads, steady! Oh, oh!" groaned the wounded man.

"Really, there seem too many men returning," said Gáltsin, again stopping the same tall soldier with the two guns. "Why are you retiring? You there, stop!"

The soldier stopped, and took off his cap with his left hand.

"Where are you going, and why?" shouted Gáltsin severely; "you scoun——"

But having come close up to the soldier, Gáltsin noticed that no hand was visible beneath the soldier's right cuff, and that the sleeve was soaked in blood to the elbow.

"I am wounded, y'r honour."

"Wounded? How?"

"Here—must 'a' been with a bullet," said the man, pointing to his arm, "but I don't know what struck my head here," and bending his head, he showed the matted hair at the back stuck together with blood.

"And whose is this other gun?"

---

[19] Our soldiera, fighting the Turks, have become so accustomed to this cry of the enemy, that they now always say that the French also shout Allah.—*L. T.*

"It's a French rifle I took, y'r honour! But I'd not have come away if it weren't to lead this fellow—he may fall," he added, pointing to a soldier who was walking a little in front, leaning on his gun, and painfully dragging his left leg.

Prince Gáltsin suddenly felt horribly ashamed of his unjust suspicions. He felt himself blushing, turned away and, neither questioning nor watching the wounded men any more, he went to the hospital.

Having pushed his way with difficulty through the porch among the wounded who had come on foot and the bearers who were carrying in the wounded and bringing out the dead, Gáltsin entered the first room, gave a look round, and involuntarily turned back and ran out into the street: it was too terrible!

VIII

The large, lofty, dark hall, lit only by the four or five candles with which the doctors examined the wounded, was literally filled. The bearers kept bringing in fresh men, laying them side by side on the floor (which was already so crowded that the unfortunates jostled one another and were soaked with each other's blood), and going to fetch more wounded. The pools of blood visible in the unoccupied spaces, the feverish breathing of several hundred men, and the perspiration of the workmen with the stretchers, filled the air with a peculiar, heavy, thick, fetid mist, in which, in different parts of the hall, the candles burnt dimly. The sound of all sorts of groans, sighs, death-rattles, now and then interrupted by shrill screams, filled the whole room. Sisters, with quiet faces, expressing not an empty, feminine, painfully tearful pity, but active, practical sympathy, here and there among the bloody coats and shirts stepped across the wounded with medicines, water, bandages, and lint. The doctors, with sleeves turned up, kneeling beside the wounded—near whom the assistants held the candles—examined, felt, and probed their wounds, not heeding the terrible groans and the prayers of the sufferers. One doctor sat at a table near the door, and at the moment Gáltsin came in was already entering No. 532.

"Iván Bogáef, Private, Company III., S— Regiment, *fractura femuris complicata!*" shouted another doctor from the end of the room, examining a shattered leg.

"Turn him over."

"Oh, oh, fathers! Oh, you're our fathers!" screamed the soldier, beseeching them not to touch him.

"Perforatio capitis!"

"Simon Nefyórdof, Lieutenant-Colonel of the N— Infantry Regiment. Have a little patience, Colonel, or it is quite impossible; I'll have to leave you!" said a third doctor, poking about with some kind of hook in the skull of the unfortunate Colonel.

"Oh, don't; oh, for God's sake be quick! be quick. Ah——!"

"Perforatio pectoris. . . . Sebastian Séreda, Private . . . what regiment? But you need not write that: *moritur.* Carry him away," said the doctor, leaving the soldier, whose eyes turned up, while the death - rattle still sounded in his throat.

About forty soldiers, stretcher-bearers, stood at the door waiting to carry the bandaged to the wards and the dead to the chapel. They looked on in silence, broken only now and then by a heavy sigh at the scene before them.

IX

On his way to the bastion Kaloúgin met many wounded; but knowing by experience that, in action, such sights have a bad effect on a man's spirits, he did not stop to question them, but, on the contrary, tried not to notice them. At the foot of the hill he met an orderly-officer galloping fast from the bastion.

"Zóbkin! Zóbkin! wait a bit."

"Yes, what?"

"Where are you from?"

"The lodgments."

"How are things there?—Hot?"

"Oh, awful!"

And the orderly galloped on.

In fact, though there was now but little small-arm firing, the cannonade had recommenced with fresh heat and persistence.

"Ah! that's bad!" thought Kaloúgin, with an unpleasant sensation, and he, too, had a presentiment, *i.e.*, a very usual thought,—the thought of death. But Kaloúgin was ambitious, and blessed with nerves of oak; in a word, he was what is called brave. He did not yield to the first feeling, but began to nerve himself. He recalled how an Adjutant, Napoleon's he thought, having delivered an order, galloped with bleeding head full speed to Napoleon.

"*Vous êtes blessé?*"[20] said Napoleon.

"*Je vous demande pardon, sire, je suis mort,*"[21] and the Adjutant fell from his horse, dead.

That seemed to him very fine, and he even a bit imagined himself to be that Adjutant Then he whipped his horse, assuming an even more dashing Cossack seat, looked back at the Cossack, who, standing up in his stirrups, was trotting behind, and rode quite gallantly up to the spot where he had to dismount. Here he found four soldiers sitting on some stones smoking their pipes.

"What are you doing there?" he shouted at them.

"Been carrying off a wounded man and sat down to rest a bit, y'r honour," said one of them, hiding his pipe behind his back and taking off his cap.

"Resting, indeed! . . . to your places, march!" and he went up the hill with them, through the trench, meeting wounded men at every step.

After ascending the hill he turned to the left, and a few steps farther on found himself quite alone. A splinter of a bomb whizzed near him, and fell into the trench. Another bomb rose in front of him and seemed flying straight at him. He suddenly felt frightened; he ran a few steps at full speed and lay down flat. When the bomb burst a considerable distance off, he felt exceedingly vexed with himself, and rose looking round to see if any one had noticed his downfall, but no one was near.

But when fear has once entered the soul it does not easily yield to any other feeling. He, who always boasted that he never even stooped, now hurried along the trench almost on all fours. He stumbled, and thought, "Oh! it's awful! they'll kill me for certain," his

---

[20] "You are wounded?

[21] "Excuse me, sir, I am dead."

breath came with difficulty, and perspiration broke out all over his body; he was surprised at himself, but no longer strove to master his feeling.

Suddenly he heard footsteps in front Quickly straightening himself, he raised his head and, boldly clanking his sabre, went on more deliberately. He could not recognise himself again. When he met a sapper-officer and a sailor, and the officer shouted to him to lie down, pointing to a bright spot which, growing brighter and brighter, approached more and more swiftly and came crashing down close to the trench, he only bent slightly, involuntarily influenced by the frightened cry, and went on.

"There's a brave 'un," said the sailor, looking quite calmly at the bomb, and at once deciding with experienced eye that the splinters could not fly into the trench, "he won't even lie down."

It was only a few steps across open ground to the bomb-proof of the Commander of the bastion, when Kaloúgin's mind again became clouded and the same stupid terror seized him; his heart beat more violently, the blood rushed to his head, and he had to constrain himself with an effort in order to run to the bombproof.

"Why are you so out of breath?" said the General, when Kaloúgin had reported his instructions.

"I walked very fast, your Excellency!"

"Won't you have a glass of wine?"

Kaloúgin drank a glass, and lit a cigarette. The action was over, only a fierce cannonade still continued from both sides. In the bomb-proof sat General N——, the Commander of the bastion, and some six other officers, among whom was Praskoúhin. They were discussing various details of the action. Sitting in this comfortable room with blue wall-paper, a sofa, a bed, a table with papers on it, a wall-clock, with a lamp burning before it, and an icón[22]—looking at these signs of habitation, at the beams more than two feet thick that formed the ceiling, and listening to the shots that here, in the bomb-proof, sounded faintly, Kaloúgin could not at all understand how he had allowed himself to be twice overcome by such unpardonable weakness. He was angry with himself, and wished for danger, in order to test his nerve once more.

"Ah! I'm glad you are here, Captain," said he to a naval officer with big moustaches who wore a Staff-Officer's coat with a St. George's Cross, and who had just entered the bomb-proof and asked the General to give him some men to repair two embrasures of his battery which had become blocked. When the General had finished speaking to the Captain, Kaloúgin said: "The Commander-in-Chief told me to ask if your guns can fire case-shot into the trenches."

"Only one of them can," said the Captain sullenly.

"All the same, let's go and see."

The Captain, who was in command of the battery, frowned and gave an angry grunt.

"I have been standing there all night, and have come in to get a bit of rest.—Couldn't you go alone?" he added. "My assistant, Lieutenant Kartz, is there, and can show you everything."

The Captain had already been more than six months in command of this, one of the most dangerous batteries. From the time the siege began, even before the bomb-proofs were erected, he had lived continuously on the bastion, and had a great reputation for

---

[22] The Russian *icóns* are paintings, in Byzantine style, of God, the Mother of God, Christ, or some saint, martyr, or angel They are usually on wood, and are often covered over, except the face and hands, with an embossed gilt cover.

courage among the sailors. That is why his refusal struck and surprised Kaloúgin. "So much for reputation," thought he.

"Well, then, I will go alone, if I may," he said in a slightly sarcastic tone to the Captain, who, however, paid no attention to his words.

Kaloúgin did not realise that whereas he had, all in all, spent some fifty hours, at different times, on the bastions, the Captain had lived there for six months. Kaloúgin was still actuated by vanity, the wish to shine, the hope of rewards, of gaining a reputation, the charm of running risks. But the Captain had already lived through all that: at first he felt vain, showed off his courage, was foolhardy, hoped for rewards and reputation, and even gained them; but now all these incentives had lost their power over him, and he saw things differently. He fulfilled his duty accurately, but, quite understanding how much the chances of life were against him after six months at the bastion, he no longer ran risks without serious need; and so the young Lieutenant, who joined the battery a week ago and was now showing it to Kaloúgin, with whom he vied in uselessly leaning out of the embrasures and climbing out on the banquette, seemed ten times braver than the Captain.

Returning to the bomb-proof after examining the battery, Kaloúgin, in the dark, came upon the General, who, accompanied by his staff officers, was going to the watch-tower.

"Captain Praskoúhin," he heard the General say, "please go to the right lodgment and tell the second battalion of the M— Regiment, which is at work there, to cease their work, leave the place, and noiselessly rejoin their regiment, which is stationed at the foot of the hill in reserve. Do you understand? Lead them yourself to the regiment."

"Yes, sir."

And Praskoúhin started at full speed towards the lodgments.

The firing was now becoming less, frequent.

X

"Is this the second battalion of the M— Regiment?" asked Praskoúhin, having run to his destination, and coming across some soldiers carrying earth in sacks.

"Just so, y'r honour!"

"Where is the Commander?"

Miháylof, thinking that the Commander of the Company was being asked for, got out of his hole and, taking Praskoúhin for a Commanding Officer, saluted, and approached him.

"The General's orders are . . . that you . . . should go . . . quickly . . . and especially quietly . . . back—no, not back, but to the reserves," said Praskoúhin, looking askance in the direction of the enemy's fire.

Having recognised Praskoúhin and made out what was wanted, Miháylof dropped his hand and passed on the order. The battalion became alert, the men took up their muskets, put on their cloaks, and set out.

No one, without experiencing it, can imagine the delight a man feels when, after three hours' bombardment, he leaves so dangerous a spot as the lodgments. During those three hours Miháylof, who more than once—and not without reason—had thought his end at hand, had had time to accustom himself to the conviction that he would certainly be killed, and that he no longer belonged to this world. But, in spite of that, he had great difficulty in keeping his legs from running away with him when, leading the company with Praskoúhin at his side, he left the lodgment.

"*Au revoir,*" said a Major, with whom Miháylof had eaten bread and cheese sitting in the hole under the breastwork, and who was remaining at the bastion in command of another battalion, "I wish you a lucky journey."

"And I wish you a lucky defence. It seems to be getting quieter now."

But scarcely had he uttered these words when the enemy, probably observing the movement in the lodgment, began to fire more and more frequently.

Our guns replied, and heavy firing recommenced.

The stars were high in the sky but shone feebly. The night was pitch dark; only the flashes of the guns and the bursting bombs made things around suddenly visible. The soldiers walked quickly and silently, involuntarily outpacing one another, only their measured footfall on the dry road was heard besides the incessant roll of the guns, the ringing of bayonets when they came in contact, a sigh, or the prayer of some poor soldier lad, "Lord, O Lord! what is it?" Now and again you heard the moaning of a man hit, and the cry "Stretchers!" (in the Company Miháylof commanded, the artillery fire alone carried off twenty-six men that night). A flash on the dark and distant horizon, the cry "Can-n-non!" from the sentinel on the bastion, and a ball flew buzzing above the Company and plunged into the earth, making the stones fly.

"What the devil are they so slow for!" thought Praskoúhin, continually looking back as he marched beside Miháylof; "I'd really better run on; I've delivered the order. . . . However, no; they might afterwards say I'm a coward! What must be, will be: I'll remain."

"Now, why is he walking with me?" thought Miháylof, on his part" I have noticed, over and over again, that he always brings ill-luck. Here it comes, I believe, straight for us."

After they had gone a few hundred paces they met Kaloúgin, who was walking briskly towards the lodgments, clanking his sabre. He had been ordered by the General to find out how the works were progressing there. But meeting Miháylof, he thought he could just as well, instead of going himself under such a terrible fire—which he was not ordered to do—find out all about it from an officer who had been there. And Miháylof giving him full details of the work, Kaloúgin, after going some way with him, turned off into a trench leading to the bomb-proof.

"Well, what news? "asked an officer who was eating his supper there all alone.

"Nothing much; it seems that the affair is over."

"Over? How's that? On the contrary, the General has just gone again to the watch-tower, and another regiment has arrived. Yes, there it is,—listen! The muskets again! Don't you go; why should you?" added the officer, noticing a movement Kaloúgin made.

"By rights I certainly ought to be there," thought Kaloúgin, "but I have already exposed myself much to-day: the firing is awful!"

"Yes, I think I'd better wait here for him," he said. And about twenty minutes later the General and the officers who were with him returned; among them was the Junker Baron Pesth, but not Praskoúhin. The lodgments had been retaken and occupied by us.

After receiving a full account of the affair, Kaloúgin, accompanied by Pesth, left the bomb-proof.

XI

"Your coat is bloody; you don't mean to say you were in the hand-to-hand fight?" asked Kaloúgin.

"Oh, it was awful! Just fancy——"

And Pesth began to relate how he led his company, how the Company-Commander was killed, how he himself stabbed a Frenchman, and how, had it not been for him, we should have lost the day.

This tale was founded on facts: the Company-Commander was killed, and Pesth had bayoneted a Frenchman, but in recounting the details the Junker invented and bragged. He bragged unintentionally, because during the whole of the affair he had been, as it were, in a fog, and so dazed that everything that happened seemed to him to have happened somehow, somewhere, and to some one. And, very naturally, he tried to recall the details in a light advantageous to himself. What really occurred was this:—

The battalion the Junker had been ordered to join for the sortie, stood for two hours under fire close to some low wall. Then the Battalion-Commander in front said something, the Company-Commanders became active, the battalion advanced from behind the breastwork, and, after going about a hundred paces, it stopped to form into company columns. Pesth was told to place himself on the right flank of the second company.

Quite unable to realise where he was and why he was there, the Junker took his place, and involuntarily holding his breath, while cold shivers ran down his back, he gazed into the dark distance, expecting something dreadful. He was, however, not so much frightened (for there was no firing) as disturbed and agitated at being in the field beyond the fortifications.

Again the Battalion-Commander in front said something. Again the officers spoke in whispers, passing on the order, and the black wall formed by the first company suddenly sank out of sight. The order was to lie down. The second company also lay down, and, in lying down, Pesth hurt his hand on a sharp prickle. Only the Commander of the second company remained standing. His short figure, brandishing a sword, moved in front of the company, and he spoke incessantly.

"Mind, lads! show them what you're made of! Don't fire, but give it them with the bayonet—the dogs! When I cry 'Hurrah,' altogether mind, that's the thing! We'll let them see who we are; we'll not shame ourselves, eh, lads? For our father the Tsar!"

"What is your Company-Commander's name?" asked Pesth of a Junker lying near him. "How brave he is!"

"Yes, he always is, in action," answered the Junker. "His name is Lisinkóvsky."

Just then a flame suddenly flashed up straight before the company, who were deafened by a resounding crash. High up in the air stones and splinters clattered. (Some fifty seconds later a stone fell from above and took a soldier's leg off.) It was a bomb fired from an elevated stand, and the fact that it reached the company showed that the French had noticed the column.

"It's bombs you're sending! Wait a bit till we get at you, then you'll taste a three-edged Russian bayonet, damn you!" said the Company-Commander, so loudly that the Battalion-Commander had to order him to hold his tongue and not make so much noise.

After that the first company rose, then the second. They were ordered to charge bayonets, and the battalion advanced.

Pesth was in such a fright that he could not in the least make out how long it lasted, where he went, or who was who. He went on as if he were drunk. But suddenly a million fires flashed from all sides, something whistled and clattered. He shouted and ran somewhere, because every one ran and shouted. Then he stumbled and fell over something. It was the Company-Commander, who had been wounded at the head of his company, and who, taking the Junker for a Frenchman, had seized him by the leg. Then, when Pesth had freed his leg and risen, some one else ran against him from behind in the dark, and nearly knocked him down again. "Run him through!" some one else shouted, "what are you stopping for?" Then some one seized a gun and stuck it into something soft. *"Ah Dieu!"* cried a dreadful, piercing voice, and Pesth only then understood that he had bayoneted a Frenchman. A cold sweat covered his whole body, he trembled as in fever, and threw down the gun. But this lasted only a moment; the thought immediately entered his head that he was a hero. He again seized the gun, and shouting "Hurrah!" ran with the crowd away from the dead Frenchman. Having run twenty paces he came to a trench. Some of our men with the Battalion-Commander were there.

"And I have killed one!" said Pesth to the Commander.

"You're a fine fellow, Baron!"

XII

"Do you know Praskoúhin is killed?" said Pesth, accompanying Kaloúgin, who was returning home.

"Impossible!"

"Yes, I saw him myself."

"Well, good-bye . . . I must be off."

"I am very pleased," thought Kaloúgin, approaching his lodgings. "It is the first time I have had such luck when on duty, it's first-rate; I am alive and well, and shall certainly get an excellent recommendation, and I am sure of a gold sabre. And I really have deserved it."

After reporting what was necessary to the General he went to his room, where Prince Gáltsin, long since returned, sat awaiting him, reading a book he had found on Kalougin's table.

It was with wonderful pleasure Kaloúgin felt himself again safe at home, and having put on his night-shirt and got into bed, he related to Gáltsin all the details of the affair, recounting them, very naturally, from a point of view from which the facts showed what a capable and brave officer he, Kaloúgin, was,—which it seemed hardly necessary to allude to, since every one knew it, and had no right or reason to question it, except, perhaps, the deceased Captain Praskoúhin, who, though he used to consider it an honour to walk arm-in-arm with Kaloúgin, had, only yesterday, told a friend privately that though Kaloúgin was a first-rate fellow, yet, between you and me, he was awfully disinclined to go to the bastions.

When Praskoúhin, walking beside Miháylof after Kaloúgin left them, had just begun to revive somewhat on approaching a safer place, he suddenly saw a bright light flash up behind him, and heard the sentinel shout "Mortar!" and a soldier walking behind him say, "That's coming straight for the bastion!"

Miháylof looked round. The bright spot seemed to have stopped at its zenith, in the position which makes it absolutely impossible to define its direction. But that only lasted a moment; the bomb—coming faster and faster, nearer and nearer, so that the sparks of its fuse were already visible and the fatal whistle audible—descended towards the centre of the battalion.

"Lie down!" shouted some one.

Miháylof and Praskoúhin lay flat on the ground. Praskoúhin, closing his eyes, only heard how the bomb crashed down on to the hard earth close by. A second passed which seemed an hour: the bomb had not exploded. Praskoúhin was afraid: perhaps he had played the coward for nothing. Perhaps the bomb had fallen far away, and it only seemed to him that its fuse was fizzing close by. He opened his eyes, and was pleased to see Miháylof lying immovable at his feet. But at that moment he caught sight of the glowing fuse of the bomb, which was spinning on the ground not a yard off. Terror—cold terror, excluding every other thought and feeling, seized his whole being. He covered his face with his hands.

Another second passed—a second during which a whole world of feelings, thoughts, hopes, and memories flashed before his imagination.

"Whom will it kill—Miháylof or me? Or both of us? And if it's me, where? In the head? then I'm done for; and if in the leg, they'll cut it off (I'll certainly ask for chloroform), and I may survive it. But perhaps only Miháylof will be killed; then I shall relate how we were going side by side, and how he was killed, and I was splashed with his blood. No, it's nearer to me . . . it will be I."

Then he remembered the twelve roubles he owed Miháylof, remembered also a debt in Petersburg that should have been paid long ago, and the gipsy song he had sung that evening. The woman he loved rose in his imagination, wearing a cap with lilac ribbons; he recollected a man who had insulted him five years ago, and whom he had not paid out; and yet, inseparable from all these, and from thousands of other recollections, the present thought, the expectation of death, did not leave him for a moment. "Perhaps it won't explode," and with desperate decision he wished to open his eyes. But at that instant a red flame pierced through the still closed lids, and with a terrible crash something struck him in the middle of his chest. He jumped up and began to run, but stumbling over the sabre that got between his legs, he fell on his side.

"Thank God, I'm only bruised!" was his first thought, and he wished to touch his chest with his hand; but his arms seemed tied to his sides, and it felt as if a vice were squeezing his head. Soldiers flitted past him, and he counted them unconsciously —"one, two, three soldiers; and there's an officer with his cloak tucked up," he thought Then lightning flashed before his eyes, and he wondered whether the shot was fired from a mortar or a cannon. "A cannon, probably. And there's another shot, and here are more soldiers—five, six, seven soldiers: they all pass by." He was suddenly seized with fear that they would crush him. He wished to shout that he was hurt, but his mouth was so dry that his tongue clove to the roof of his mouth, and a terrible thirst tormented him. He felt it wet about his chest; and this sensation of being wet made him think of water, and he longed to drink even this that made him feel wet "I suppose I hit myself in falling and bled," thought he, and giving way more and more to fear lest the soldiers who kept flitting past might trample on him, he gathered all his strength and tried to shout "Take me with you!" but instead of that he uttered such a terrible groan that he was frightened to hear it. Then some other red fires began dancing before his eyes, and it seemed to him that the soldiers put stones on him; the fires danced less and less, but the stones they put on him pressed more and more heavily. He made an effort to push off the stones—stretched himself—and saw and heard and felt nothing more. He had been killed on the spot by a bomb-splinter in the middle of his chest.

XIII

When Miháylof saw the bomb and fell down, he too, like Praskoúhin, lived through an infinitude of thoughts and feelings in the two seconds that passed before the bomb burst. He prayed mentally, and repeated, "Thy will be done." And at the same time he thought, "Why did I enter the army? and why did I join the infantry to take part in the campaign? Would it not have been better to have remained with the Uhlan regiment at T——, and spent my time with my friend Natasha? And now here I am," . . . and he began to count "one, two, three, four," deciding that if the bomb burst at an even number he would live, but if at an odd number he would be killed. "It is all over, I'm killed," he thought when the bomb burst (he did not remember whether at an odd or even number), and he felt a blow and a cruel pain in his head. "Lord, forgive me my trespasses!" he muttered, folding his hands; he rose, but fell on his back senseless.

When he came to, his first sensation was that of the blood trickling down his nose and the pain in his head, which was much less violent. "That's the soul passing," he thought. "How will it be *there*? Lord! receive my soul in peace. . . . Only it's strange," thought he, "that, dying, I should hear so distinctly the steps of the soldiers and the sounds of the firing."

"Bring stretchers! Eh, the Captain is killed!" shouted a voice above his head, which he involuntarily recognised as the voice of the drummer, Ignátyef.

Some one took him by the shoulders. With an effort he opened his eyes, and saw the sky above him, the groups of stars, and two bombs racing one another as they flew above him. He saw Ignátyef, soldiers with stretchers and guns, the embankment, the trenches, and suddenly realised that he was not yet in the other world.

He was slightly wounded in the head by a stone. His first feeling was one almost of regret: he had prepared himself so well and calmly to go *there*, that the return to reality, with its bombs, stretchers, and blood seemed unpleasant. The second feeling was unconscious joy at being alive; and the third a wish to get away from the bastion as quickly as possible. The drummer tied a handkerchief round his Commander's head, and taking his arm led him towards the Ambulance Station.

"But why, and where, am I going?" thought the Lieutenant-Captain when he had collected his senses. "My duty is to remain with the company, and not to leave it behind, especially," whispered a voice, "as the company will soon be out of range of the guns."

"Never mind, my lad," said he, drawing away his hand from the attentive drummer, "I won't go to the Ambulance Station, but will stay with the company.

And he turned back.

"It would be better to have it properly bandaged, your honour," said Ignátyef. "It's only the heat of the moment makes it seem nothing; mind it don't get worse, and just see what warm work it is here. . . . Really, your honour——"

Miháylof stood for a moment undecided, and would probably have followed Ignátyef's advice had he not reflected how many severely wounded there must be at the Ambulance Station. "Perhaps the doctors will smile at my scratch," thought the Lieutenant-Captain, and in spite of the drummer's arguments he returned to his company.

"And where is Staff-Officer Praskoúhin, who was with me?" he asked, when he met the Ensign who was leading the company.

"I don't know; killed, I think," replied the Ensign unwillingly.

"Killed? or wounded? How is it you don't know? wasn't he going with us? And why did you not bring him away?"

"How could we under such a fire?"

"Ah! what have you done, Michael Ivánitch?" said Miháylof angrily. "How could you leave him if he's alive? Even if he's dead his body ought to have been brought away."

"Alive indeed, when I tell you I myself went up and saw him!" said the Ensign. "Excuse me, it's hard enough to collect our own. . . . There they are, the villains," added he, "it's cannon balls they're sending now!"

Miháylof sat down and held his head, which ached terribly when he moved. "No, it is absolutely necessary to go back and fetch him; he may still be alive," said Miháylof. "It is our *duty*, Michael Ivánitch."

Michael Ivánitch did not answer.

"There now! he did not take him at the time, and now soldiers will have to be sent back by themselves . . . and how can one send them? Under this terrible fire they may be killed uselessly," thought Miháylof.

"Lads! some one will have to go back to fetch the officer who was wounded out there in the ditch," said he, not very loudly or peremptorily, feeling how unpleasant it would be for the soldiers to execute this order. And so it was. As he had not named any one in particular no one came forward to obey the order.

"And, after all, he may be dead already: it is not worth while exposing men uselessly to such danger. It's all my fault, I ought to have seen to it. I will go back myself and find out whether he is alive. It is my *duty*," said Miháylof to himself.

"Michael Ivánitch! you lead the company, I'll catch you up," said he, and lifting his cloak with one hand, while with the other he kept touching a small icón of St. Metrophanes that hung round his neck and in which he had great faith, he ran quickly along the trench.

Having convinced himself that Praskoúhin was dead, Miháylof dragged himself back panting, his hand holding the bandage that had slipped on his head, which now again ached badly. When Miháylof overtook the battalion, it was already at the foot of the hill, and almost beyond the range of the shots. I say 'almost,' because a stray bomb now and then came even here.

"To-morrow I had better go and be entered at the Ambulance Station," thought the Lieutenant-Captain, while a medical assistant, who had turned up, was bandaging his head.

XIV

Hundreds of bodies, freshly stained with blood, of men who, two hours before, had been filled with various lofty and trivial hopes and wishes, lay with stiffened limbs on the dewy, flowery valley between the bastions and the parallels, and on the smooth floor of the Mortuary Chapel in Sevastopol. Hundreds of men, with prayers and curses on their parched lips, crawled, writhed, and moaned, some among the corpses in the flowery valley, others on stretchers, on beds, and on the bloody floor of the Ambulance Station! And, just as on other days, the dawn appeared over the Sapoún hill, the twinkling stars paled, the white mist rose above the dark roaring sea, the rosy morning glow lit up the east, the long purple clouds travelled across the blue horizon, and, just as on other days, promising joy, love and happiness to all the awakening world, in power and glory rose the sun.

XV

The next evening the Chasseurs' band was again playing on the boulevard, and again officers, junkers, soldiers, and young women promenaded round the pavilion and along the side-walks under the sweet, white, blooming acacias.

Kaloúgin, Prince Gáltsin, and a Colonel were walking arm-in-arm near the pavilion and talking of last night's affair. The main clue to the talk, as always in such cases, was not the affair itself but the part the speaker had taken in it Their faces and tones were serious, almost sorrowful, as if the losses of the night had touched and saddened every one of them. But, to tell the truth, as none of them had lost any one very dear to him, this sorrowful expression was only an official one they considered it their duty to exhibit

Kaloúgin and the Colonel, though they were first-rate fellows, were, in fact, ready to see such an affair every day if they could have a gold sword, and be made Major-General each time. It is very well to call some conqueror a monster because he destroys millions to gratify his ambition. But go and ask any Ensign Petroúshef or Sub-Lieutenant Antónof, on their conscience, and you will find that every one of us is a little Napoleon, a little monster, ready to start a battle and kill a hundred men, only to get an extra medal or one-third additional pay.

"No, I beg pardon," said the Colonel," it began first on the left side. *I was there myself."*

"Well, perhaps," said Kaloúgin, "*I spent more time on the right. I went there twice, first to look for the General, and then just to see the lodgments. That's where it was hot!"*

"Kaloúgin must know," said Gáltsin. "By the way, V—— told *me* to-day that you are a trump——"

"But the losses, the losses are terrible!" said the Colonel "*In my regiment me had four hundred casualties. It is astonishing that I am still alive."*

Just then the figure of Miháylof, with his head bandaged, appeared at the end of the boulevard and came towards these gentlemen.

"What, are you wounded, Captain?" said Kaloúgin.

"Yes, slightly, with a stone," answered Miháylof.

"*Est-ce que le pavillon est baissé déja?"*[23] asked Prince Gáltsin, glancing at the Lieutenant-Captain's cap, and not addressing any one in particular.

"*Non, pas encore,"*[24] answered Miháylof, who wished to show that he understood and spoke French.

"Do you mean to say the truce still continues?" said Gáltsin, politely addressing him in Russian, and thereby intimating (so it seemed to the Lieutenant-Captain): 'It must, no doubt, be difficult for you to have to speak French, so hadn't we better simply . . .' and thereupon the Adjutants left him. The Lieutenant-Captain again felt exceedingly lonely, as he had done the day before. After bowing to various people—some of whom he did not wish, and some of whom he did not venture to join—he sat down near Kazársky's monument and smoked a cigarette.

Baron Pesth also turned up on the boulevard. He related that he had been present at the parley, and how he had spoken with the French officers. According to his account, one of them had said to him, *"Sil n'avait pas fait clair encore pendant une demi-heure,*

---

[23] "Has the flag of truce been lowered yet?
[24] "No, not yet."

les embuscades auraient été reprises,"[25] and he replied, *"Monsieur! je ne dis pas non, pour ne pas vous donner un démenti,"*[26] and he told how well it had come out, etc. etc.

In reality, though he had been at the parley, he had not managed to say anything particular, though he much wished to speak with the French (for it's awfully jolly to speak with those fellows). Junker Baron Pesth had long paced up and down the line asking the Frenchmen near to him, *"De quel régiment êtes-vous?"*[27] He got his answer and nothing more. When he went too far beyond the line, the French sentry, not suspecting that "that soldier" knew French, abused him in the third person singular:" *Il vient regarder nos tra-vaux, ce sacré——"*[28] In consequence of which Junker Baron Pesth, finding nothing more to interest him at the parley, rode home, and on his way back composed the French phrases he was now repeating.

Captain Zóbof, who spoke so loud, was on the boulevard, the shabbily - dressed Captain Obzhógof, the artillery captain who never curried favour with any one, a Junker fortunate in his love affairs,—all the same faces as the day before, and all with the same recurring motives.

Only Praskoúhin, Nefyórdof, and a few more were missing, and hardly any one now remembered or thought of them, though there had not been time for their bodies to be washed, laid out, and put into the ground.

XVI

On our bastions and on the French parallels white flags are hung out, and between them in the flowery valley lie heaps of bootless, mangled corpses, clad in grey and blue, which workmen are removing and piling on to carts. The air is filled with the smell of decaying corpses. From Sevastopol and from the French camp crowds of people have poured out to see the sight, and with eager and amicable curiosity draw near one another.

Listen to what these people are saying to each other.

Here, in a circle of Russians and Frenchmen who have collected round him, a young officer, who speaks French badly but sufficiently to be understood, is examining a Guardsman's pouch.

"Eh sussy, poor quah se waso lié?"[29]

"Parce que c'est une giberne d'un régiment de la garde, Monsieur, qui porte l'aigle impérial."[30]

"Eh voo de la guard?"[31]

"Pardon, Monsieur, du 6-ème de ligne."[32]

"Eh sussy oo ashtay?"[33] pointing to a cigarette-holder of yellow wood in which the Frenchman is smoking a cigarette.

"A Balaclava, Monsieur! C'est tout simple en bois de palme."[34]

---

[25] "Had it remained dark for another half-hour, the ambuscades would have been recaptured."

[26] "Sir, I will not say no, lest I give you the lie."

[27] "What regiment do you belong to?"

[28] "He's come to look at our works, the confounded——"

[29] "And this, what is this tied bird for?"

[30] "Because this is a cartridge pouch of a Guard regiment, monsieur, and bears the Imperial eagle."

[31] "And do you belong to the Guards?"

[32] "No, monsieur, to the 6th Regiment of the line."

[33] "And this: where did you buy?"

[34] "At Balaclava, Monsieur! It's only made of palm wood."

"Joli,"[35] says the officer, guided in his remarks not so much by his own free will as by the French words he knows.

"Si vous voulez bien garder cela comme souvenir de cette rencontre, vous m'obligerez."[36]

And the polite Frenchman puts out his cigarette and presents the holder to the officer with a slight bow. The officer gives him his, and all present, both Frenchmen and Russians, smile and seem pleased.

Here is a brisk infantry-man in a pink shirt, with cloak thrown over his shoulders, accompanied by others who stand by him, with their hands at their backs, and merry, inquisitive faces. He approaches a Frenchman and asks a light for his pipe. The Frenchman draws at, and stirs up the tobacco in his own short pipe, and shakes a light into that of the Russian.

"Tabac boon?" says the soldier in the pink shirt, and the spectators smile. "Oui, *bon tabac, tabac turc,*" says the Frenchman. *"Chez vous autre tabac—Russe? bon?"*

"Roos boon," says the soldier in the pink shirt, while the onlookers shake with laughter. *"Fransay* not *boon, bong jour mossier!"* says the soldier in the pink shirt, letting off his whole stock of French at once, and he slaps the Frenchman on the stomach and laughs. The French also laugh.[37]

"Ils ne sont pas jolis ces b—— de Russes," says a Zouave among the French.

"De quoi de ce qu'ils rient donc?"[38] says another, a dark man with an Italian accent, coming up to our men.

"Coat *boon,*" says the cheeky soldier, examining the embroidery of the Zouave's coat; and everybody laughs again.

"Ne sors pas de ta ligne, à vos places, sacré nom!"[39] cries a French Corporal, and the soldiers separate with evident unwillingness.

And here, amidst a group of French officers, is one of our young cavalry officers gushing. They are talking about some Count Sazónof, *"que j'ai beaucoup connu, Monsieur,"* says a French officer with only one epaulet—*"c'est un de ces vrais comtes russes, comme nous les aimons."*[40]

"Il y a un Sazónof, que j'ai connu," says the cavalry officer, *"mais il n'est pas comte, à moins, que je sache, un petit brun de voire âge à peu prés."*[41]

"C'est ça, Monsieur, c'est lui. Oh! que je voudrais le voir, ce cher comte. Si vous le voyez, je vous prie bien de lui faire mes compliments—Capitaine Latour,"[42] he said, bowing.

---

[35] "Pretty."

[36] "If you will be so good as to keep it as a souvenir of this meeting, you will do me a favour."

[37] "They are not handsome, these d——Russians."

[38] "What are they laughing about?"

[39] "Don't leave your ranks; to your places, damn it!"

[40] "Whom I knew very intimately, Monsieur. He is one of those real Russian Counts, of whom we are so fond."

[41] "I am acquainted with a Sazónof, but he is not a Count, as far as I know,—a small, dark man, of about your age."

[42] "Just so, Monsieur, that is he. Oh! how I should like to meet the dear Count! If you should see him, please be so kind as to give him my compliments—Captain Latour."

"N'est-ce pas terrible la triste besogne, que nous faisons? Ça chauffait cette nuit, n'est-ce pas?"[43] said the cavalry officer, wishing to maintain the conversation and pointing to the corpses.

"Oh, Monsieur, c'est affreux! Mais quels gaillards vos soldats, quels gaillards! C'est un plaisir, que de se baltre avec des gaillards comme eux."[44]

"Il fait avouer que les vólres ne se mouchent pas du pied non plus,"[45] said the cavalry officer, bowing, and imagining himself to be very agreeable.

But enough.

Let us rather look at this ten-year-old boy in the old cap (probably his father's), with shoes on his stocking-less feet, and nankeen trousers held by one brace. At the very commencement of the truce he came over the entrenchments, and ever since he has been walking about the valley, looking with dull curiosity at the French and at the corpses that lie on the ground, and gathering the blue flowers with which the valley is strewn. Returning home with a large bunch of flowers he holds his nose to escape the smell which is borne towards him by the wind, and stopping near a heap of corpses collected together, he gazes long at a terrible, headless body which lies nearest to him. After standing there some time, he draws nearer and touches with his foot the stiff, outstretched arm of the corpse. The arm trembles a little. He touches it again more boldly; it moves, and falls back again to its old position. The boy gives a sudden scream, hides his face in his flowers, and runs towards the fortifications as fast as his legs can carry him.

Yes, white flags are on the bastions and on the parallels; the flowery valley is covered with dead bodies; the beautiful sun is sinking towards the blue sea; and the undulating blue sea glitters in the golden rays of the sun. Thousands of people crowd together, look at, speak to, and smile at one another. And these people—Christians confessing the one great law of love and self-sacrifice—looking at what they have done, do not at once fall repentant on their knees before Him who has given them life and laid in the soul of each a fear of death and a love of good and of beauty, and do not embrace like brothers with tears of joy and happiness

The white flags are lowered, again the engines of death and suffering are sounding, again innocent blood flows, and the air is filled with moans and curses.

There, I have said what I wished to say this time. But a painful hesitation seizes me. Perhaps I ought to have left it unsaid. Perhaps what I have said belongs to that class of evil truths which, unconsciously hidden within the souls of each one, should not be uttered for fear of becoming injurious, as the dregs in the bottle must not be shaken for fear of spoiling the wine.

Where in this tale is the evil shown that should be avoided? Where is the good that should be imitated? Who is the villain, who the hero of the story? All are good, and all are bad.

Not Kaloúgin, with his brilliant courage—*bravoure de gentilhomme*—and the vanity which influences all his actions; not Praskoúhin, the empty, harmless fellow (though he fell in battle for faith, throne, and fatherland); not Miháylof, with his shyness; nor Pesth, a child without firm principles or convictions,—can be either the villain or the hero of a tale.

---

[43] "Is it not terrible, this sad duty we are engaged in? It was warm work last night, was it not?"

[44] "Ah, Monsieur, it is terrible! But what fine fellows your men are, what fine fellows! It is a pleasure to fight with fellows of that make."

[45] "It must be admitted that yours are no fools either."

The hero of my tale, whom I love with all the power of my soul, whom I have tried to portray in all his beauty, who has been, is, and will be beautiful—is Truth.

AUGUST 1855

Towards the end of August, between Douvánka[46] and Bahtchisaráy, through the hot, thick dust of the rocky and hilly highway, an officer's trap was slowly toiling towards Sevastopol (that peculiar kind of trap you never meet anywhere else, something between a Jewish *brítchka*, a Russian cart, and a basket).

In the front of the trap, pulling at the reins, squatted an orderly in a nankeen coat and wearing a cap that had once belonged to an officer but was now quite limp: behind, on bundles and bales covered with a soldier's cloak, sat an infantry officer in a summer cloak. The officer, as far as one could judge while he was sitting, was not tall, but was very broad and massive, not so much across the shoulders as from back to chest. His neck and the back of his head were much developed and very solid. He had not what we call a waist, nor was he at all stouter round the stomach: on the contrary, he was rather lean, especially in the face, which was burnt to an unwholesome yellow. He would have been good-looking had it not been for a certain puffiness, and for the broad, soft; wrinkles, not due to age, which blurred the outlines of his features, making them seem larger and giving the face a general look of coarseness and lack of freshness. His small eyes were hazel, with a daring and even insolent expression: he had very thick but not broad moustaches, the ends of which were bitten off, and his chin, and especially his jaws, were covered with an exceedingly strong, thick, black, two-days-old beard.

This officer had been wounded in the head by a bomb splinter on the 10th of May and still wore a bandage; but having felt well again for the last week, he had left the hospital at Simferópol and was now on his way to rejoin his regiment, stationed somewhere in the direction whence the firing came—but whether in Sevastopol itself, on the North Side, or at Inkerman, no one had yet been able to tell him for certain. Already the frequent firing, especially at times when no hills intercepted it and when the wind carried it this way, sounded exceedingly distinct, and seemed quite near. Now an explosion shook the air and made one start involuntarily; now sounds less loud followed each other in quick succession like the roll of drums, broken now and then by a startling boom; now again all these sounds mingled into a kind of rolling crash, like peals of thunder when a storm is raging in all its fury and rain has just begun to fall in torrents. Every one was saying (and besides one could hear for oneself) that a terrific bombardment was going on. The officer kept telling his orderly to drive faster; he seemed in a hurry to get to his destination. They met a train of Russian peasants' carts that had taken provisions to Sevastopol, and were now on their way back loaded with sick and wounded soldiers in grey uniforms, sailors in black cloaks, volunteers with red fezzes on their heads, and bearded militiamen. The officer's trap had to stand still in the thick, motionless cloud of dust raised by this train of carts, and the officer, frowning and, blinking while his eyes filled with dust, sat looking at the faces of the sick and wounded who were passing.

"There's a soldier of our company, that one who is so weak," said the Orderly, turning to his master and pointing to a cart loaded with wounded men then just passing them.

A bearded Russian with a felt hat sat sideways in the front of the cart plaiting the lash of a whip, the handle of which he held to his side with his elbow. Behind him in the

---

[46] The last posting-station north of Sevastopol.—L. T.

cart five or six soldiers, lying and sitting in different positions, were being jolted along. One, with a bandaged arm and his cloak thrown loosely over his shirt, though he looked pale and thin, sat upright in the middle of the cart and raised his hand as if to salute the officer, but remembering, probably, that he was wounded, pretended he only meant to scratch his head. A man lay beside him on the bottom of the cart, of whom all that was visible was his two hands holding on to the sides of the cart, and his lifted knees swaying this way and that like rags. A third, with a swollen face and with a soldier's cap shaking on the top of his bandaged head, sat sideways with his feet hanging out, and, leaning his elbows on his knees, seemed to be dozing. The officer addressed him: "Dolzhnikóf!" he cried;

"Here!" said the soldier, opening his eyes and taking off his cap, and answering in such a loud, abrupt bass that it sounded as if twenty soldiers had shouted all together.

"When were you wounded, lad?"

The soldier's leaden eyes with their swollen lids brightened up; he had evidently recognised his officer.

"Good-day, y'r 'onor!" said the soldier in the same abrupt bass.

"Where is your regiment stationed now?"

"In Sevastopol. We were going to move on Wednesday, y'r 'onor!"

"Where to?"

"Don't know, y'r 'onor—to the North Side, maybe.—Now they're firing right across, y'r 'onor," he added in a long-drawn tone, replacing his cap: "mostly bombs—they reach right across the bay. *He's* giving it us awful hot now . . ."

What the soldier said further could not be heard, but the expression of his face and his bearing showed that his words, spoken with the bitterness of one suffering, were not reassuring.

The officer in the trap, Lieutenant Kozeltsóf, was not an every-day sort of man. He was not one of those who live and act this way or that because others live and act so; he did what he liked, and others followed his example, and felt sure it was right. He had a nature endowed with many minor gifts: he could sing well, played the guitar, talked smartly and wrote very easily (especially official papers, the knack of writing which he had gained when he was adjutant of his battalion); but the most remarkable characteristic of his nature was his ambitious energy, which, though chiefly founded on those same minor talents, was in itself a marked and striking feature. He had ambition of a kind most often found in male circles, especially military, and this had become so much a part of his life that he could imagine no other line than to dominate or to perish. Ambition was at the root even of his inward impulses, and in his private thoughts he liked to put himself first when he compared himself with others.

"It's likely I should pay attention to the chatter of a Tommy!" muttered the Lieutenant, with a feeling of heaviness and apathy at heart and a certain dimness of thought, left by the sight of the convoy of wounded men, and by the words of the soldier, enforced as they were by the sounds of the cannonade.

"Funny fellow that Tommy! Now then, Nikoláyef, get on! . . . are you asleep?" he added rather fretfully, as he arranged the skirt of his cloak.

Nikoláyef jerked the reins, clicked his tongue, and the trap rolled on at a trot

"We'll only stop just to feed the horse, and then we'll go on at once: to-day," said the officer.

II

At the entrance to a street of remains of ruined stone Tartar houses in Douvánka, Lieutenant Kozeltsóf was stopped by a convoy of bombs and cannon-balls on its way to Sevastopol, which blocked the road.

Two foot-soldiers sat on the stones of a ruined wall in the midst of a cloud of dust eating a water-melon and bread.

"Going far, comrade?" asked one of them, with his mouth full of bread, as another soldier with a little bag on his back stopped near them.

"Going to join our regiment," answered the soldier, looking past the water-melon and readjusting his bag: "We have been nigh on three weeks in the province looking after hay for our company, but now we've all been recalled, but we don't know where the regiment is. Some say it crossed to the Korábelnaya last week. Perhaps you have heard, good people?"

"In the town, friend, it's quartered in the town," muttered the other, an old convoy soldier, who was digging with a clasp-knife into an unripe, whitish water-melon. "We've only come from there since noon. Ah, it's awful there, my lad!"

"How so, good people?"

"Why, can't you hear? They're firing from all sides to-day, there's not a place left whole. As for the likes of us as has been killed—there's no counting 'em!" And making an expressive gesture with his hand the speaker put his cap straight.

The soldier who had stopped shook his head meditatively and clicked his tongue, then he took a pipe out of his boot-leg, and, without filling it, merely loosened the scorched tobacco in it, and lit a bit of tinder at the pipe of one of the soldiers. Then he raised his cap and said—

"One can't get away from God, good people! Forgive me." And straightening his bag with a jerk he went his way.

"Ah, it would be far better to wait!" said with conviction he who was digging into the water-melon.

"It all comes to the same!" muttered the soldier, squeezing between the wheels of the crowded carts.

III

The posting-station was full of people when Kozeltsóf drove up. The first person he met in the porch was a very young, lean man, the superintendent, bickering with two officers who were following him.

"It's not three days, but maybe ten you'll have to wait . . . even generals have to wait, sirs!" said the superintendent, wishing to hurt the travellers' feelings: "I can't harness myself for you, can I?"

"Then don't give horses to anybody if you have none! Why did you give them to that lackey with the baggage?" shouted the elder of the officers, who had a tumbler of tea in his hand.

"Just consider a moment, Mr. Superintendent," said the other, a very young officer, hesitatingly: "we are not going for our own pleasure. You see we too must be needed there, since we are summoned. I shall really have to report it to the General. It will never do, you know . . . you, it seems, don't respect an officer's position."

But the elder interrupted him crossly. "You always spoil everything! You only hamper me; one must know how to speak to these people. There now, he has lost all respect. . . . Horses, I say, this very minute!"

"Willingly, my dear sir, but where am I to get them from?"

The superintendent was silent for a few moments. Then he suddenly flared up, and waving his arms he began:—

"I know it all very well, my dear sir, and fully understand it, but what's one to do? You give me but" (a ray of hope appeared on the faces of the officers) . . . "let me but hold out to the end of the month, and I'll remain here no longer. I'd rather go to the Maláhof Hill than remain here, I swear I would! Let them do what they please. There's not one sound vehicle in the whole place, and it's the third day the horses haven't had a wisp of hay." And the superintendent disappeared behind the gate.

Kozeltsóf entered the room together with the officers.

"Well," said the elder very calmly to the younger, though the moment before he had seemed quite beside himself, "we've been three months on our way already; let's wait a little longer. Where's the harm? there's time enough!"

The dirty, smoky room was so full of officers and trunks that Kozeltsóf with difficulty found a seat on the window-sill. While observing the faces and listening to the conversation of the others, he began making himself a cigarette. To the right of the door, round a crooked, greasy table on which two *samovárs* stood with verdigris showing here and there, and sugar lay on various bits of paper, sat the principal group. A young moustacheless officer in a new quilted Caucasian coat was filling a teapot, and there were four other such young officers in different parts of the room. One of them with some kind of a fur coat rolled up under his head, was sleeping on the sofa; another was standing cutting up some roast mutton for a one-armed officer who was sitting at the table. Two officers, one in an Aide-de-camp's cloak, the other in infantry uniform made of fine cloth, and with a satchel across his shoulders, were sitting by the stove; and the way they looked at the others, and the manner in which the one with the satchel smoked his cigarette, proved that they were not infantry officers of the line, and were glad they were not. Their manner did not show contempt, but rather a certain calm self-satisfaction, founded partly on money and partly on intimacy with generals—a consciousness of superiority reaching even to a desire to conceal it Then there was a thick-lipped young doctor, and an artillery officer who looked like a German—these were sitting on the sofa, almost on the feet of the sleeping officer, counting money. There were also several orderlies, some dozing, others busy with bundles and trunks near the door. Among all these people Kozeltsóf did not recognise a single acquaintance; but he listened with interest to their conversation. The young officers, who, as he at once concluded from their appearance, had come straight from a training-college, pleased him, and reminded him of the fact that his brother, who was also coming straight from the training-college, ought, in a few days' time, to reach one of the batteries in Sevastopol. But he did not like the officer with the satchel, whose face he had seen somewhere before—everything about him seemed insolent and repulsive. And thinking, "We'll put him down if he ventures to say anything," the Lieutenant even moved from the window to the stove, and sat down there. Belonging to a line regiment, and being a good officer, he, in general, did not like those "of the Staff," and such he at once knew these officers to be.

IV

"I say, isn't it an awful nuisance that we're so near and still can't get there," said one of the young officers. "There may be an action to-day and we shan't be in it."

The piping voice and the fresh rosy spots which appeared on his face betrayed the sweet, youthful bashfulness of one in constant fear that his words may come out wrong.

The officer who had lost an arm looked at him with a smile.

"You will get there quite soon enough, believe me," he said.

The young man looked with respect at the armless officer—whose emaciated face unexpectedly lit up with a smile—and became silently absorbed in making his tea. And, really, the face, the attitude, and especially the empty sleeve of the officer, expressed a kind of calm indifference, that seemed to reply to every word and action: "All this is excellent, all this I know, and all this I can do if I only wish to."

"Well, and how shall we decide it?" the young officer began again, turning to his comrade in the Caucasian coat "Shall we stay the night here, or go on with our own horse?"

His comrade decided to stay.

"Just fancy, Captain," continued he who was making the tea, addressing the one-armed officer and handing him a knife he had dropped, "we were told that horses were awfully dear in Sevastopol, so we two bought one together in Simferópol."

"I expect they made you pay a stiff price."

"I really don't know, Captain; we paid ninety roubles for it and the trap. Is that very much?" he said, turning to the company in general, including Kozeltsóf, who was looking at him.

"It's not much if it's a young horse," said Kozeltsóf.

"You think so? . . . And we were told it was too much. Only it limps a bit, but that will pass. We were told it's strong."

"What training-college are you from?" asked Kozeltsóf, who wished to get news of his brother.

"We are now from the Nobles' Regiment. There are six of us, and we are all going to Sevastopol—at our own desire," said the talkative young officer: "only we don t know where our battery is: some say it is in Sevastopol, but those fellows there say it is in Odessa."

"Couldn't you find out in Simferopol?" Kozeltsóf asked.

"They didn't know. . . . Just fancy, one of our comrades went to the Chancellery there and got nothing but rudeness. Just fancy how unpleasant! Would you like a ready-made cigarette?" he said to the one-armed officer, who was trying to get out his cigar-case.

He attended to this officer's wants with a kind of servile enthusiasm.

"And are you also from Sevastopol?" he continued. "Oh dear, how wonderful it is! How we all in Petersburg used to think about all of you and all our heroes!" he said, addressing Kozeltsóf with respect and cordial endearment.

"Well, then you may find you have to go back?" asked the Lieutenant

"That's just what we are afraid of. Just fancy, when we had bought the horse and got all that we needed—a coffee-pot with a spirit-lamp and other necessary little things—we had no money at all left," he said in a low tone, glancing at his comrade, "so that if we have to return we don't at all know how we shall manage."

"Didn't you receive your travelling allowance, then?" asked Kozeltsóf.

"No," answered the young officer in a whisper; "they only promised to give it us here."

"Have you the certificate?"

"I know that a certificate is the principal thing, but when I was at his house, a senator in Moscow—he is my uncle—told me that I should get one here; or else he would have given it me himself. But will they give me one in Sevastopol?"

"Certainly they will."

"And I also think I shall get one there," he said in a tone which proved that, having asked the same question at some thirty other posting-stations, and having everywhere received different answers, he no longer quite believed any one.

V

"Who ordered soup?" demanded the rather dirty landlady, a fat woman of about forty, as she came into the room with a tureen of cabbage-soup.

The conversation immediately stopped, and every one in the room fixed their eyes on the landlady. One officer even winked to another, with a glance at her.

"Oh, Kozeltsóf ordered it," said the young officer. "He'll have to be woke up. . . . Get up for dinner!" he said, stepping to the sofa and shaking the sleeper's shoulder. A lad of about seventeen, with merry black eyes and very rosy cheeks, jumped up energetically and stepped into the middle of the room rubbing his eyes.

"Oh, I beg your pardon," he said to the doctor, against whom he had knocked in rising.

Lieutenant Kozeltsóf recognised his brother at once and went up to him.

"Don't you know me?" he asked with a smile.

"Ah-a-a!" cried the younger Kozeltsóf, "this is wonderful!" and he began kissing his brother.

They kissed three times, but hesitated before the third kiss, as if the thought, "Why has it to be just three times?" had struck both of them.

"Well, I *am* glad!" said the elder, looking into his brother's face: "come out into the porch and let's have a talk."

"Come, come along. I don't want any soup: you eat it, Féderson," he said to his comrade.

"But you wanted to eat."

"I don't want any."

Out in the porch the younger one kept asking his brother, "Well, and how are you? Tell me how things are," and saying how glad he was to see him, but did not tell him anything about himself.

After five minutes, when they had found time to be silent a little, the elder brother asked why the younger had not entered the Guards, as every one had expected.

"I wanted to get to Sevastopol as soon as possible. You see, if things turn out well here, one can get on quicker than in the Guards; there it takes ten years to become a Colonel, and here in a year Todlében from a lieutenant-colonel has become a general. And if one gets killed—well, it can't be helped."

"So that's the sort of stuff you are made of!" said his brother, with a smile.

"But that's nothing. The chief thing, you know, brother," said the younger, smiling and blushing as if he were going to say something very shameful—"the chief thing was that somehow one's ashamed to be living in Petersburg, while here men are dying for the Fatherland. And besides, I wished to be with you," he added, still more shyly.

The elder did not look at him. "How odd you are!" he said, and took out his cigarette-case. "Only the pity is that we shall not be together."

"I say, tell me quite frankly: is it very dreadful at the bastions?" suddenly asked the younger.

"It seems dreadful at first, but one gets used to it You'll see for yourself"

"Yes, another thing. Do you think they will take Sevastopol? I think they won't; I am certain they won't"

"Heaven only knows."

"It's so provoking. . . . Just think, what a misfortune: do you know, we've had a whole bundle of things stolen on the way, and my shako was inside, so that I am in a terrible position. Whatever shall I appear in?"

Kozeltsóf *secundus*, Vladímir, was very like his brother Michael, but it was the likeness of an opening rose-bud to a withered dog-rose. He had the same fair hair as his brother, but it was thick, and curled about his temples, and a little tail of it grew down the delicate white nape of his neck—a sign of luck according to the nurses. The delicate white skin of his face was not always flushed, but the full young blood, rushing to it, betrayed every movement of the soul. He had the same eyes as his brother, but more open and brighter, which was especially noticeable because a slight moisture often made them glisten. Soft, fair down was beginning to appear on his cheeks and above the red lips, on which a shy smile often played, disclosing the white, glistening teeth. Straight, broad-shouldered, the uniform over his red Russian shirt unbuttoned—as he stood there in front of his brother, cigarette in hand, leaning against the banisters of the porch, his face and attitude expressing naive joy, he was such a pleasantly pretty boy that one could not help wishing to look and look at him. He was very pleased to see his brother, and looked at him with respect and pride, imagining him to be a hero; but in some respects, namely, in what in society is considered good form—being able to speak good French, knowing how to behave in the presence of people of high position, dancing, etc., he was rather ashamed of his brother, looked down on him, and even hoped, if possible, to educate him. All his impressions, so far, were from Petersburg, especially from the house of a lady who liked nice-looking lads, with whom he used to spend his holidays, and from the house of a senator in Moscow, where he had once danced at a grand ball.

VI

Having talked almost their fill, and reached a feeling which often comes when two people find there is little in common between them though they are fond of each other, the brothers remained silent for some time.

"Well, then, collect your things and let us be off," said the elder.

The younger suddenly blushed and became confused.

"Do we go straight to Sevastopol? "he asked, after a moment's silence.

"Well, of course. You have not got much luggage, I suppose; we'll get it all in."

"All right! let's start at once," said the younger with a sigh, and went towards the room.

But he stopped in the passage without opening the door, hung down his head sorrowfully and began thinking.

"Now, at once, straight to Sevastopol within reach of the bombs . . . terrible! Ah well, never mind; it had to be sooner or later. And now, at least, it's with my brother ..."

The thing was, that only now, at the thought that once seated in the trap he would reach Sevastopol before again alighting, and that there were no more chances of anything detaining him, did he clearly realise the danger he had been seeking; and the thought of its nearness staggered him. Having calmed himself as well as he could, he entered the room; but a quarter of an hour passed and he did not return to his brother, so the latter at last opened the door to call him. The younger Kozeltsóf, standing like a guilty schoolboy, was speaking with an officer. When his brother opened the door he seemed quite disconcerted.

"Yes, yes, I'm just coming," he cried, waving his hand to prevent his brother coming in. "Please wait for me there."

A few minutes later he came out and approached his brother with a deep sigh. "Just fancy," he said; "it turns out that I can't go with you, brother."

"What? what nonsense!"

"I'll tell you the whole truth, Mísha . . . None of us have any money left, and we are all in debt to that Lieutenant-Captain whom you saw in there. It's such a shame!"

The elder brother frowned, and remained silent for a considerable time.

"Do you owe much?" he asked at last, looking at his brother from under his brows.

"Much? No, not very much; but I feel terribly ashamed. He paid for me at three post-stations, and the sugar was always his, so that I don't . . . Yes, and we played at *preférence* . . . and I lost a little to him."

"That's bad, Volódya! Now what would you have done if you had not met me?" the elder remarked sternly, without looking at him.

"Well, you see, brother, I thought I'd pay when I got my travelling allowance in Sevastopol. I could do that, couldn't I? . . . So I'd better drive on with him to-morrow."

The elder brother drew out his purse and with slightly trembling fingers produced two ten-rouble notes and one of three roubles.

"There's the money I have," he said; "how much do you owe?"

Kozeltsóf did not speak quite truly when he made it appear as if this were all the money he bad. He had four gold coins sewn into the cuff of his sleeve in case of special need, but he had resolved not to touch them.

It turned out that Kozeltsóf *secundus* only owed eight roubles, including the sugar and the *preference*. The elder brother gave them to him, only remarking that it would never do to go playing *preference* when one has no money.

"How high did you play?"

The younger did not reply. The question seemed to suggest a doubt of his honour. . . . Vexed with himself, ashamed of having done something that could give rise to such suspicions, and hurt at such offensive words from the brother he so loved, his impressionable nature suffered so keenly that he did not answer. Feeling that he could not suppress the sobs which were gathering in his throat, he took the money without looking at it and returned to his comrades.

VII

Nikoláyef, who had strengthened himself in Douvánka with two cups of *vódka*[47] sold by a soldier he had met on the bridge, kept pulling at the reins, and the trap jumped along the stony, and here and there shady, road that leads by the Belbéc to Sevastopol. The two brothers, with their legs touching as they jolted along, sat in obstinate silence, though they never ceased to think about each other.

"Why did he offend me?" thought the younger. "Could he not have left that unsaid? Just as if he thought me a thief: and I think he is still angry, so that we have gone apart for good. And how fine it would have been for us to be together in Sevastopol! Two brothers, friends with one another, fighting the enemy side by side: one, the elder, not highly educated but a brave warrior, and the other, young, but . . . also a fine fellow . . . In a week's time I would have proved to everybody that I am not so very young! I shall leave off blushing, and my face will look manly; my moustaches, too, will have grown by that time—not very big, but quite sufficient," and he pulled at the short down that showed at the corners of his mouth. "Perhaps when we get there to-day we may go straight into action, he and I together. And I'm certain he must be steadfast and very brave; a man who says little but does more than others. I wonder whether or not he is pushing me to the very edge of the trap on purpose. He surely feels that I am uncomfortable, and pretends not to notice me." He continued his meditation, pressing to the edge of the seat, and afraid to stir lest his brother should notice that he was uncomfortable: "So we'll get there to-day, and then, maybe, straight to the bastion; I with the guns, and brother with his company, both together. Then supposing the French come down on us, I shall fire and fire. I kill quite a lot of them, but they still keep coming straight at me. I can no longer fire, and of course there is no escape for me; but suddenly ray brother rushes to the front with his sword drawn, and I seize a musket and we run on with the soldiers. The French attack my brother: I run forward, kill one Frenchman, then another, and save my brother. I am wounded in one arm; I seize the gun in the other hand and still run on. Then my brother falls at my side, shot dead by a bullet. I stop for a moment, bend sadly over him, draw myself up and cry, 'Follow me; we will avenge him! I loved my brother more than anything on earth,' I shall say, 'I have lost him. Let us avenge him; let us annihilate the foe or let us all die here!' They will all rush shouting after me. Then all the French army, with Pélissier himself, will advance. We shall slaughter them, but at last I shall be wounded a second and a third time, and shall fall down dying. Then all will rush to me and Gortchakóf himself will come and ask if I want anything. I shall say that I want nothing—only to be laid near my brother: that I wish to die beside him. They will carry me and lay me down by the blood-stained corpse of my brother. I shall raise myself and say only, 'Yes, you did not know how to value two men who really loved the Fatherland: now they have both fallen. May God forgive you!' and then I'll die."

Who knows how much of these dreams will come true?

"I say, have you ever been in a hand-to-hand fight?" he suddenly asked, having quite forgotten he was not going to speak to his brother.

"No, never," answered the elder. "We lost two thousand from the regiment, but it was all at the fortifications, and I also was wounded there. War is not carried on at all in the way you imagine, Volódya."

---

[47] *Vódka* is a spirit distilled from rye. It is the commonest form of strong drink in Russia.

The pet name Volódya touched the younger brother. He longed to put matters right with the elder, who had no idea that he had given offence.

"You are not angry with me, Mísha?" he asked after a minute's pause.

"Angry? What for?"

"Oh, nothing . . . only because of what passed . . .

it's nothing."

"Not at all," answered the elder, turning towards him and slapping him on the knee.

"Then forgive me if I have pained you, Mísha." And the younger brother turned away to hide the tears that suddenly filled his eyes.

VIII

"Can this be Sevastopol already?" asked the younger brother when they reached the top of the hill.

Spread out before them they saw the Roadstead with the masts of the ships, the sea with the enemy's fleet in the distance, the white shore batteries, the barracks, the aqueducts, the docks, and the buildings of the town, the white and purple clouds of smoke that, rising constantly from the yellow hills surrounding the town, floated in the blue sky, lit up by the rosy rays of the sun, which was reflected brilliantly in the sea, towards whose dark horizon it was already sinking.

Volódya looked without the slightest trepidation at the dreadful place that had so long been in his mind: he even gazed with concentrated attention at this really splendid and unique sight, feeling aesthetic pleasure and an heroic sense of satisfaction at the thought that in another half-hour he would be there; and he continued gazing until, on the North Side, they came to the commissariat of his brother's regiment, where they had to ascertain the exact position of the regiment and of the battery.

The officer in charge of the commissariat lived near the so-called 'new town' (a number of wooden sheds constructed by the sailors' families) in a tent connected with a good-sized shed constructed of green oak branches that had not yet had time to dry completely.

The brothers found the officer seated at a dirty table on which stood a tumbler of cold tea, a tray with a *vódka* bottle, and bits of dry caviare and bread. He sat in a dirty yellowish shirt, counting, with the aid of a big abacus, an enormous pile of bank-notes. But before speaking of the personality of this officer and his conversation, we must examine the interior of the shed more attentively, and see something of his way of living and his occupations. His new-built shed was as big, as strongly wattled, and as conveniently arranged with tables and seats made of turf, as though it were built for a general or the commander of a regiment. To keep the dry leaves from falling in, the top and sides were lined with three carpets, which, though hideous, were new, and must have cost money.

On the iron bedstead which stood beneath the most striking carpet (depicting a lady on horseback), lay a bright red velvet-pile bedcover, a torn and dirty pillow, and a raccoon fur-lined overcoat. On the table were a looking-glass in a silver frame, an exceedingly dirty silver-backed hair-brush, a broken horn comb full of greasy hair, a silver candlestick, a bottle of liqueur with an enormous red and gold label, a gold watch with a portrait of Peter I., two gold pens, a box of some kind of capsules, a crust of bread, and a scattered pack of old cards. Bottles, full and empty, were stowed away under the bed. This officer was in charge of the regimental commissariat and of the forage for the horses. With him lived his great friend, the commissioner employed on contracts. When the brothers entered, the latter was asleep in the tent, while the commissary officer was making up the regimental accounts for the month. The officer had a very handsome and military appearance: tall, with large moustaches and a portly figure. What was unpleasant about him was only a certain moistness and a puffiness about his face that almost hid his small grey eyes (as if he were filled with porter), and his extreme lack of cleanliness, from his thin greasy hair to his big bare feet slipped into some kind of ermine-lined slippers.

"What a heap of money!" said Kozeltsóf *primus* on entering the shed, as he fixed his eyes eagerly on the pile of bank-notes. "Ah, if you'd lend me but half, Vasíly Miháylovitch!"

The commissary officer shrank back a little, recognised his visitor, and, gathering up the money, bowed without rising.

"Oh, if it were mine! It's Government money, my dear fellow. . . . And who is that with you?" he said, putting the money into a cash-box that stood near him, and looking at Volódya.

"It's my brother, straight from the training-college. We've come to learn from you where our regiment is stationed."

"Take a seat, gentlemen. Won't you have something to drink? A glass of porter, perhaps?" he said, and without taking any further notice of his visitors he rose and went out into the tent

"I don't mind if I do, Vasíly Miháylovitch."

Volódya was struck by the grandeur of the commissary officer, his off-hand manner, and the respect with which his brother addressed him.

"I expect this is one of their best officers, whom they all respect—probably simple-minded, but hospitable and brave," he thought as he sat down modestly and shyly on the sofa.

"Then where is our regiment stationed?" shouted the elder brother across to the tent

"What?"

The question was repeated.

"Seifert was here this morning: he says the regiment has gone over to the Fifth Bastion." "Is that certain?"

"If I say so, of course it's certain. However, the devil only knows if he told the truth! He'd not take much to tell a lie either. Well, will you have some porter?" said the commissary officer, still speaking from the tent

"Well, yes, I think I will," said Kozeltsóf.

"And you, Ósip Ignátyevitch, will you have some?" continued the voice from the tent, apparently addressing the sleeping contractor. "Wake up; it's past four."

"Why do you bother one? I'm not asleep," answered a thin voice lazily.

"Well, get up, it's dull without you," and the commissary officer came out to his visitors.

"A bottle of Simferópol porter!" he cried.

The orderly entered the shed with an expression of pride as it seemed to Volódya, and in getting the porter from under the seat he jostled Volódya.

The bottle of porter had been emptied, and the conversation had continued for some time in the same strain, when the flap of the tent opened, and out stepped a rather short, fresh-looking man in a blue dressing-gown with tassels, and a cap with a red band and a cockade. He came twisting his little black moustaches and looking somewhere in the direction of one of the carpets, and answered the greetings of the officers with a scarcely perceptible movement of his shoulders.

"I think I'll also have a glass," he said, sitting down to the table.

"Is it from Petersburg you've come, young man?" he remarked, addressing Volódya in a friendly manner. "Yes, sir, and I'm going to Sevastopol." "At your own request?"

"Yes, sir."

"Now, what do you do it for, gentlemen? I don't understand it," remarked the commissioner. "I'd be ready to walk to Petersburg on foot, I think, if they'd let me go. My word, I'm sick of this damned life!"

"What have you to complain of?" asked the elder Kozeltsóf, "as if you were not well enough off here."

The contractor gave him a look and turned away.

"The danger, privations, lack of everything," continued he, addressing Volódya. "And what induces you to do it? I do not at all understand you, gentlemen. If you got any profit out of it; but no. Now would it be nice, at your age, to be crippled for life?"

"Some want to make a profit and others serve for honour's sake," said the elder Kozeltsóf crossly, again intervening in the conversation.

"Where's the honour of it if you have nothing to eat?" said the contractor, laughing disdainfully and addressing the commissary officer, who also laughed. "Wind up and let's have the tune from *Lucia,*" he said, pointing to the music-box; "I like it"

"What sort of a fellow is that Vasíly Miháylovitch?" asked Volódya when he had left the shed with his brother in the dusk of the evening and they were driving to Sevastopol.

"So-so, only terribly stingy. But that contractor, I can't bear to look at. . . . I'll give him a thrashing some day."

IX

It was almost night when they reached Sevastopol. Driving towards the large bridge across the Roadstead Volódya was not exactly dispirited, but his heart felt heavy. All he had seen and heard was so different from his past, still recent, experiences—the large, light, parquet-floored examination hall, the jolly, friendly voices and laughter of his comrades, the new uniform, the beloved Tsar, whom he had been accustomed to see for the last seven years, and who at parting from them had, with tears in his eyes, called them his children—and all he saw now was so little like his beautiful, radiant, high-souled dreams.

"Well, here we are," said the elder brother when they reached the Michael Battery and dismounted from their trap. "If they let us cross the bridge we will go at once to the Nicholas Barracks. You can stay there till the morning, and I'll go to the regiment and find out where your battery is and come for you to-morrow."

"Oh, why? Let's go together," said Volódya. "I'll go to the bastion with you. It doesn't matter; one must get used to it sooner or later. If you go, so can I."

"Better not."

"No, please. I shall at least find out how . . ."

"My advice is, don't go; but however . . ."

The sky was clear and dark; the stars, the ever-moving fire of the bombs, and the flash of the guns already showed up brightly in the darkness. The large white building of the battery, and the beginning of the bridge,[48] loomed out in the darkness. Literally every second, several artillery shots and explosions ever more loudly and distinctly shook the air in quick succession. Through this roar, and as if answering it, came the dull murmur of the Roadstead. A slight breeze blew in from the sea and the air smelled moist. The brothers reached the bridge. A recruit, awkwardly striking his gun against his hand, called out, "Who goes there?"

"Soldier!"

"No one's allowed to pass!"

"How is that? We must."

"Ask the officer."

The officer, who was sitting on an anchor dozing, rose and ordered that they should be allowed to pass.

"One may go there, but not back."

"Where are you driving, all of a heap!" he shouted to the regimental waggons, which, laden high with gabions, were crowding the entrance.

As the brothers were descending to the first pontoon, they came upon some soldiers going in the opposite direction and talking loudly.

"If he's had his outfit money his account is squared—that's so."

"Eh, lads," said another, "when one gets to the North Side one sees light again. My word! it's different air altogether."

"Get along," said the first "Why, the other day a damned shot came flying here and tore off two soldiers' legs for them, so that ..."

Waiting for the trap, the brothers, after crossing the first pontoon, stopped on the second, on to which the waves washed here and there. The wind, which seemed gentle on land, was strong and gusty here; the bridge swayed, and the waves broke noisily against beams, anchors, and ropes, and washed over the boards. To the right, the sea, divided by a smooth, endless black line from the starry, light, bluish-grey horizon, roared dark, misty, and hostile. Far off in the distance gleamed the lights of the enemy's fleet. To the left loomed the black bulk of one of our ships, against the sides of which the waves beat audibly. A steamer, too, was visible, moving quickly and noisily from the North Side. The flash of a bomb exploding near the steamer lit up, for a moment, the gabions piled high on its deck, two men standing on the paddle-box, and the white foam and splash of the greenish waves cut by the vessel. On the edge of the bridge, his feet dangling in the water, sat a man in his shirt repairing the pontoon. In front, above Sevastopol, the same fires were flying, and louder and louder came the terrible sounds. A wave flowing in from the sea washed over the right side of the bridge and wetted Volódya's boots, and two soldiers passed by him splashing their feet through the water. Suddenly something came crashing down which lit up the bridge ahead of them, a cart driving over it, and a horseman; and bomb fragments fell whistling and splashing into the water.

"Ah, Michael Semyonitch[49]!" said the rider, stopping his horse in front of the elder Kozeltsóf, "have you recovered?"

---

[48] This pontoon bridge was erected daring the summer of 1855. At first it was feared that the water was too rough in the Roadstead for a secure bridge to be built, but it served its purpose and even stood the strain put upon it by the retreat of the Russian army to the North Side,

[49] In addressing any one in Russian, it is usual to employ the christian name and patronymic: i.e., to the christian name (in this case Michael) the father's christian name is joined (in this case Semyón), with the termination vitch (o-vitch or e-vitch), which means, "son of." The termination is often shortened to itch. Surnames are less used than in English, for the patronymic is suitable for all circumstances of life—both for

"As you see. And where is fate taking you?"

"To the North Side for cartridges. You see, I'm taking the place of the regimental adjutant to-day. . . . We are expecting an attack from hour to hour."

"And where is Mártsof?"

"His leg was torn off yesterday while he was sleeping in his room in town. . . . Did you know him?"

"Is it true the regiment is now at the Fifth Bastion?"

"Yes; we have taken the place of the M——regiment You'd better call at the Ambulance; you'll find some of our fellows are there; they'll show you the way."

"Well, and my lodgings in the Morskáya Street, are they safe?"

"Eh, my dear fellow! they've long since been shattered by the bombs. You'll not know Sevastopol again; not a woman left, not a restaurant, no music: the last brothel left yesterday. It's melancholy enough now. Good-bye!"

And the officer trotted away.

Terrible fear suddenly overcame Volódya; he felt as if a ball or a bomb-splinter would come at once and hit him straight on the head. The damp darkness, all these sounds, especially the murmur of the splashing water—all seemed to tell him to go no farther, that no good awaited him here, that he would never again set foot on this side of the bay, that he should turn back at once and run somewhere, as far as possible from this dreadful place of death. "But perhaps it is too late, it is already now decided," thought he, shuddering partly at the idea and partly because the water had soaked through his boots and was wetting his feet

Volódya sighed deeply and moved a few steps from his brother.

"O Lord! shall I really be killed—just I? Lord, have mercy on me!" he whispered, and made the sign of the cross.

"Well, Volódya, come!" said the elder brother when the trap had driven on to the bridge. "Did you see the bomb?"

On the bridge the brothers met carts loaded with wounded men, with gabions, and one with furniture driven by a woman. No one stopped them at the further side.

Keeping instinctively under the wall of the Nicholas Battery, and listening to the bombs that were here bursting overhead and to the howling of the falling fragments, the brothers came silently to that part of the battery where the icón hangs. Here they heard that the Fifth Light Artillery, to which Volódya was appointed, was stationed at the Korábelnaya,[50] and they decided that Volódya, in spite of the danger, should spend the night with his elder brother at the Fifth Bastion, and go from there to his battery next morning. After turning into a corridor and stepping across the legs of the soldiers who lay sleeping all along the wall of the battery, they at last reached the Ambulance Station.

---

speaking to and of any one—except where people on very intimate terms use only the christian name, or a pet name. (See also Preface, pp. xiv, and xv.)

[50] The Korábelnaya was a suburb of Sevastopol lying to the east of the South Bay and to the south of the Roadstead. Like the "North Side," it was connected with Sevastopol by a floating bridge. (See map.) cap, was walking with her hands in her apron pockets by the side of the elder woman, and seemed afraid of being left behind.

X

Entering the first room, lined with beds on which wounded men were lying, and the air of which was permeated with a horribly disgusting hospital smell, they met two Sisters of Mercy just going out

One, a woman of fifty, with black eyes and a stern expression, was carrying bandages and lint and giving orders to a young lad, a medical assistant, who was following her. The other, a very pretty girl of about twenty, whose pale, tender, fair face looked with a peculiarly sweet helplessness from under her white

Kozeltsóf asked them if they knew where Mártsof was, whose leg had been torn off the day before.

"He is of the P—— regiment, I think?" asked the elder. "Is he a relation of yours?"

"No, a comrade."

"Take them to him," said she in French to the young Sister. "It is this way," and she herself, followed by the assistant, went to one of the patients.

"Come along; what are you looking at?" said Kozeltsóf to Volódya, who stood with raised brows and a look of suffering on his face, unable to tear his eyes from the wounded. "Come now!"

Volódya followed his brother, but still kept looking back and repeating unconsciously, "O my God! my God!"

"I suppose he has not been here long?" the Sister remarked to Kozeltsóf, with reference to Volódya, who followed them along the corridor with exclamations and sighs.

"He has only just come."

The pretty Sister looked at Volódya, and suddenly began to cry.

"My God! my God! when will it end?" she said, with despair in her voice.

They entered the officers' ward. Mártsof was lying on his back, his sinewy arms, bare to the elbow, thrown behind his head, and an expression on his yellow face as of a man who has clenched his teeth to keep himself from screaming with pain. His sound leg with a stocking on showed from under the blanket, and one could see the toes moving spasmodically.

"Well, how are you?" asked the Sister, raising his slightly bald head with her slender delicate fingers (on one of which Volódya noticed a gold ring) and arranging his pillow.

"In pain, of course!" he answered angrily. "That'll do—the pillow's all right!" and the toes in the stocking moved still faster. "How d'you do? What's your name?"—"Excuse me," he said, when Kozeltsóf had told him. "Ah yes, I beg pardon! one forgets everything here. Why, we lived together," he added, without any sign of pleasure, and looked inquiringly at Volódya.

"This is my brother, arrived to-day from Petersburg."

"H'm! And I have got my discharge," said the wounded man, frowning. "Oh, how it hurts; if only it would be over quicker."

He drew up his leg and, moving his toes still more rapidly, covered his face with his hands.

"He must be left alone," said the Sister in a whisper, while tears filled her eyes: "he is very ill."

While yet on the North Side the brothers had decided to go to the Fifth Bastion together, but on leaving the Nicholas Battery it was as though they had agreed not to expose themselves to needless danger, and, without mentioning the matter, they decided to go each his own way.

"Only, how will you find it, Volódya?" said the elder. "Look here! Nikoláyef shall take you to the Korábelnaya, and I'll go on alone and come to you to-morrow."

Nothing more was said at this last parting between the brothers.

XI

The thunder of the cannonade continued with unabated violence. Ekateríninskaya Street, down which Volódya walked, followed by the silent Nikoláyef, was quiet and deserted. In the dark he could distinguish only the broad street with white walls of large houses, many of which were in ruins, and the stone pavement along which he was walking. Now and then he met some soldiers and officers. As he was passing by the left side of the Admiralty Building a bright light inside showed him the acacias planted along the sidewalk of the streets, with green stakes to support them, and sickly, dusty leaves. He distinctly heard his own footsteps and those of Nikoláyef, who followed him breathing heavily. He was not thinking of anything: the pretty Sister of Mercy, Mártsof s foot with the toes moving in the stocking, the darkness, the bombs, and different images of death, floated dimly before his imagination. The whole of his young, impressionable soul was weighted down and crushed by a sense of loneliness, and of the general indifference shown to his fate in these dangerous surroundings. "I shall be killed; I shall suffer, endure torments, and no one will shed a tear!" And all this in place of the hero's life, full of energy and evoking sympathy, that had figured in his beautiful dreams. The bombs burst and whistled nearer and nearer. Nikoláyef sighed more and more often but did not speak. As they were crossing the bridge that led to the Koràbelnaya he saw a whistling something fall, and disappear into the water nearby, lighting for a second the lilac waves to a flaming red, and then come splashing up again.

"Look there! it was not extinguished," said Nikoláyef in a hoarse voice.

"Yes," answered Volódya, in an involuntarily high-pitched, plaintive tone which surprised him.

They met wounded men carried on stretchers, and more carts loaded with gabions; on the Korábelnaya they met a regiment, and men on horseback rode past One of these was an officer followed by a Cossack. He was riding at a trot; but seeing Volódya he stopped his horse near him, looked in his face, turned away, and, touching his horse with the whip, rode on.

"Alone, alone! no one cares whether I exist or not," thought the lad, and felt inclined to cry in real earnest

At the top of the hill, past a high wall, he entered a street of small shattered houses continually lit up by the bombs. A dishevelled, tipsy woman, coming out of a gate with a sailor, knocked up against Volódya.

"Then if he'sh a man o' 'onor," she muttered—"pardon y'r exshensh offisher!"

The poor lad's heart ached more and more. On the dark horizon the lightnings flashed more and more frequently, and the bombs whistled and exploded more and more often around them. Nikoláyef sighed, and suddenly began to speak in an awe-restrained tone, as it seemed to Volódya.

"There now, and we were in such a hurry to get here! Always push on and push on! This is a fine place to hurry to!"

"Well, but if my brother had recovered his health," answered Volódya, hoping by conversation to disperse the dreadful feeling that had seized him.

"Health indeed! Where's his health when he's quite ill? Even them as is really well had best lie in hospital these times. Not much pleasure to be got All you get is to have a leg or arm carried off! It's done before you know where you are! Here, even in the town, what horrors! but what's it like at the *bak-sions!* One says all the prayers one knows going there. See the beastly thing how it twangs past you!" he added, listening to the buzzing of a flying fragment

"Now," continued Nikoláyef, "I'm to show y'r honor the way. Our business is in course to obey orders: what's ordered has to be done; but the trap's been left with some Tommie or other, and the bundle's untied. . . . 'Go! go!' but if something's lost, why Nikoláyef answers for it!"

After a few steps more, they came to the square. Nikoláyef was silent, but kept sighing.

Then he said suddenly, "There, y'r honor, there's where your *antillary's* stationed. Ask the sentinel, he'll show you."

Again a few steps, and Volódya no longer heard Nikoláyef sighing behind him. Then he suddenly felt himself quite, utterly, alone. This sense of loneliness, face to face, as it seemed to him, with death, pressed like a heavy, cold stone on his heart. He stopped in the midst of the square, glanced round to see if any one were looking, grasped his head and thought with horror—

"O Lord! am I really a vile, miserable coward . . . when it's for my Fatherland, for the Tsar, for whom I used to long to die? No! I am a miserable, wretched being!" And Volódya, filled with despair and disappointed with himself, asked the sentinel the way to the house of the Commander of the battery and went where he was directed.

XII

The dwelling of the Commander of the battery, which the sentinel showed him, was a small two-storied house with an entrance from the yard. The faint light of a candle shone through a window patched up with paper. An orderly sat on the steps smoking his pipe. He went in to inform the battery Commander of Volódya's arrival, and then showed him into the room. In the room, under a broken mirror between two windows, stood a table littered with official papers, and there were several chairs, and an iron bedstead with clean bedding and a little rug beside it.

Just at the door stood a handsome man with large moustaches, a sergeant-major, wearing his side-arms and with a cross and an Hungarian medal[51] on his uniform. A staff-officer, a short man of about forty, in a thin old cloak and with a swollen cheek tied round with a bandage, was pacing up and down the room.

"I have the honour to report myself, Ensign Kozeltsóf 2nd, ordered to join the 5th Light Artillery," said Volódya on entering the room, repeating the sentence he had been taught.

The Commander answered his greeting dryly, and, without shaking hands, asked him to take a seat.

---

[51] That is, a medal granted for service in the suppression of the Hungarian rising in 1849, when Nicholas I. supported Austria.

Volódya sat down shyly on a chair by the writing table, and began playing with a pair of scissors his hand happened to fall on. The Commander, with his hands at his back and with drooping head, continued to pace the room in silence as if trying to remember something, only now and then glancing at the hand that was playing with the scissors.

The Commander was a rather stout man, with a large bald patch on his head, thick moustaches hanging straight down over his mouth, and pleasant, hazel eyes. His hands were well shaped, clean and plump, his small feet were much turned out, and he trod with firmness and in a way that indicated that the Commander of the battery was not a diffident man.

"Yes," he said, stopping opposite the Sergeant-major, "the ammunition horses must have an extra peck, beginning from to-morrow; they are getting very thin. Don't you think so?"

"All right! one can add it, your honour? Oats are a bit cheaper now," answered the Sergeant-major, standing at attention, but moving his fingers, which evidently liked to help his conversation by gestures. "Then our forage-master, Frantchúk, sent me a note from the convoy yesterday that we must be sure, y'r excellency, to buy axles there; they say they can be got cheap. Will you give the order?"

"Well, let him buy them—he has money," and the Commander again began to pace the room. "And where are your things?" he asked, suddenly stopping in front of Volódya.

Poor Volódya was so overcome by the thought that he was a miserable coward, that he seemed to see contempt for himself as such in each look and word. He felt as if the Commander of the battery had already discerned his secret and was chaffing him. He was abashed, and replied that his things were at the Gráfskaya, and that his brother had promised to send them on next day.

The Commander did not stop to hear him out, but, turning to the Sergeant-major, asked, "Where could we put up the Ensign?"

"The Ensign, sir?" said the Sergeant-major, making Volódya still more confused by casting a rapid glance at him, which seemed to ask, "What sort of an Ensign is that?"

"Why, downstairs, your Excellency. We can put his honour up in the Lieutenant-Captain's room;" he continued after a moment's thought; "the Lieutenant-Captain is at the *bakston* at present, so there's his bed empty."

"Well, then, if you don't mind for the present," said the Commander. "I should think you are tired, and we'll make better arrangements to-morrow."

Volódya rose and bowed.

"Would you like a glass of tea?" said the Commander of the battery when Volodya had nearly reached the door; "the *samovár* can be lit"

Volódya bowed and went out The Orderly showed him downstairs into a bare, dirty room, where, with all sorts of rubbish lying about, stood a bed without sheets or blankets, on which, covered with a thick cloak, a man in a pink shirt was sleeping. Volódya took him for a soldier.

"Peter Nikoláyitch," said the Orderly, shaking the sleeper by the shoulder, "the Ensign will sleep here . . . This is our Yunker," he added, turning to Volódya.

"Oh, please don't let me disturb you!" said Volódya; but the Yunker, a tall, solid young man, with a handsome but very stupid face, rose from the bed, threw the cloak over his shoulders, and, evidently not yet awake, left the room saying, "Never mind; I shall lie down in the yard."

XIII

Left alone with his thoughts, Volódya's first feeling was one of fear at the disorderly, cheerless state of his own soul. He longed to fall asleep and forget all that surrounded him, but especially himself. Putting out the candle, he took off his cloak and lay down on the bed; and to get rid of the darkness, of which he had been afraid from childhood upwards, he drew the cloak over his head. But suddenly the thought occurred to him that now, immediately, a bomb would crash through the roof and kill him, and he began to listen. Just above his head he heard the steps of the Commander of the battery.

"If it does come," he thought, "it will first kill those upstairs and then me—anyway not me alone." This thought comforted him a little, and he was about to fall asleep.

"But supposing that all of a sudden, to-night, Sevastopol is taken, and the French break in here? What shall I defend myself with?" He rose and went up and down the room. The fear of real danger drove away the fanciful fear of the darkness. A saddle and a *samovár* were the only hard things in the room.

"What a wretch I am—a coward, a despicable coward!" he thought again, and once more the oppressive feeling of contempt, even disgust of himself, came over him, He lay down again, and tried not to think.

Then, under the influence of the unceasing noise, which made the panes rattle in the one window of the room, the impressions of the day rose up in his imagination, reminding him of danger. Now he seemed to see wounds and blood, then bombs and splinters flying into the room, then the pretty Sister of Mercy bandaging his wounds and crying over him as he lies dying, then his mother seeing him off in the little country town, and praying fervently with tears in her eyes before the wonder-working icon—and again sleep seemed impossible. But suddenly the thought of God the Almighty, who could do anything and hears every prayer, came clearly into his mind. He knelt down, crossed himself, and folded his hands as he had been taught to do when a child. This attitude suddenly brought back to him an old, long-forgotten sense of comfort

"If I must die, if I must cease to exist, then do it, Lord," he thought, "do it quickly; but if courage is needed, and firmness, which I lack, give them me. Deliver me from the shame and disgrace which are more than I can bear, and teach me what I must do to fulfill Thy will."

The frightened, cramped, childish soul suddenly matured, brightened, and became aware of new, bright, and broad horizons. He thought and felt many things during the short time this state continued, but soon fell into a sweet untroubled sleep, amid the continued booming of the cannonade and the rattle of the window panes.

O Lord Almighty! Thou alone hast heard and knowest the simple yet burning and desperate prayers of ignorance, of confused repentance, prayers for bodily health and for spiritual enlightenment, that have risen to Thee from this dreadful place of death: from the General, who, an instant after his mind has been absorbed by the Order of St George upon his neck, with trepidation feels the nearness of Thy presence, to the private soldier prostrate on the bare floor of the Nicholas Battery, who prays for the future reward he dimly expects for all his sufferings.

XIV

The elder Kozeltsóf, happening to meet a soldier of his regiment in the street, went with him straight to the Fifth Bastion.

"Keep to the wall, your honour!" said the soldier.

"Why?"

"It's dangerous, your honour: there it is, flying over us," said the soldier, listening to the sound of a ball that whistled past and fell on the hard ground on the other side of the road.

Here were still the same streets, the same or even more frequent firing, the same sounds, the same groans from the wounded one met on the way, and the same batteries, breastworks, and trenches, as when he was in Sevastopol in the spring; but somehow it now all seemed more melancholy and yet more energetic. There were more holes in the houses, no lights in any of the windows except those of Koústchin's house (a hospital), not a woman to be seen; and the place no longer bore its former customary character and air of unconcern but seemed burdened with heavy suspense and weariness.

But the last trench is reached, there is the voice of a soldier of the P—— regiment who has recognized his former Company Commander, and there stands the third battalion, pressing against the wall in the darkness, and now and then lit up for an instant by the firing; and sounds are heard of subdued talking and the clatter of muskets.

"Where is the Commander of the regiment?" asked Kozeltsóf.

"In the naval-officers' casemate, your honour," answers an obliging soldier; "let me show you the way."

Passing from trench to trench, the soldier led the way to a little ditch within a trench. A sailor sat in the ditch smoking a pipe. Behind him was a door, through a chink in which a light shone.

"Can I go in?"

"I'll announce you directly," and the sailor went in at the door.

Two voices were heard talking inside.

"If Prussia remains neutral," said one voice, "Austria will also . . ."

"What matters Austria," said the other, "when the Slavonic lands . . . Well, ask him in."

Kozeltsóf had never been in this casemate and was struck by its elegance. It had a parquet floor and a screen in front of the door. Two beds stood against the walls; in one of the corners there was a large icón, the Mother of God, with an embossed gilt cover, and a pink lamp burned before her. On one of the beds a naval officer, quite dressed, was lying asleep. On the other, before a table on which stood two uncorked bottles of wine, sat the speakers—the new regimental commander and his adjutant. Though Kozeltsóf was far from being a coward, and was not in the least guilty of any offence against either the government or the Regimental Commander, yet he felt abashed in the presence of his former comrade the Colonel, so proud was the bearing of that Colonel when he rose and listened to Kozeltsóf.

"It's strange," thought Kozeltsóf, as he looked at his Commander, "it is only seven weeks since he took the command, and now all his surroundings—his dress, manner, looks,—already show the power of a regimental commander. It is not long since this same Batrístchef used to hobnob with us, wore one and the same dark cotton print shirt the whole week, ate the rissoles and dumpling every day, never inviting any one!—but look at him now! What a look of cold pride in his eyes! It seems to say: 'Though, being a Commander of the new school, I am your comrade, yet, believe me, I know very well that you'd give half your life to be in my place!'"

"You have been under treatment a long time," said the Colonel, with a cold look at Kozeltsóf.

"I have been ill, Colonel! The wound is not thoroughly closed even now."

"Then it's a pity you have come," said the Colonel, looking suspiciously at the officer's full figure. "But still, you are capable of taking duty?"

"Certainly, sir, I am."

"Well, sir, I am very glad. Then you'll take over from Ensign Záytsef the Ninth Company, that you had before. You will receive your orders at once."

"Yes, sir."

"Be so good, when you go, as to send the regimental adjutant to me." The Commander finished with a slight bow, thereby intimating that the audience was at an end.

On leaving the casemate, Kozeltsóf muttered something to himself several times and shrugged his shoulders, as if he were hurt, or uncomfortable, or provoked—and provoked, not with the Colonel (he had no grounds), but with himself; and he felt dissatisfied with everything around him.

XV

Before going to join the officers, Kozeltsóf went to greet his company, and to see where it was stationed. The breastworks of gabions, the plan of the trenches, the cannon he passed, and even the fragments and bombs he stumbled over on the way, all lit up incessantly by the flashes of the firing, were quite familiar to him. All this had vividly impressed itself on his memory three months before, when he had spent two consecutive weeks at this same bastion. Though there was much that was dreadful in the recollection, yet there was some charm of old times mixed with it, and he recognised all the familiar places and objects with pleasure, as if the fortnight spent here had been a pleasant one. His company was stationed against the wall of defence on the side towards the Sixth Bastion.

Kozeltsóf entered a long bomb-proof, quite open on the entrance side, where he was told he would find the Ninth Company. There was literally no room to put one's foot in the whole bomb-proof: it was crowded with soldiers from the very entrance. At one side burned a crooked tallow candle, which a soldier who was lying on the ground held over the book another was reading from, spelling out the words. Round the candle could be seen in the dim light heads uplifted in eager attention to the reader. The book was a primer, and on entering the bomb-proof Kozeltsóf heard the following:

"Pra-yer af-ter les-sons. We thank Thee, O Cre-a-tor . . ."

"Snuff the candle!" said a voice. "It's a fine book."

"Oh-my-God," . . . continued the reader.

When Kozeltsóf asked for the Sergeant-major the reader stopped, and the soldiers began moving, coughing, and blowing their noses, as is usual after a restrained silence. The Sergeant-major, buttoning his uniform, rose from near the reader's group, and stepping over and on to the legs of those who, for want of room, were unable to move them, he came to the officer.

"Good evening, friend! Is this the whole of our company?"

"We wish your honour health. Welcome back, your honour!" answered the Sergeant-major with a cheerful and friendly look at Kozeltsóf. "How is your health getting on, your honour? Thank God, you're better! We have been missing you!"

It was easy to see that Koseltsóf was liked by his company.

Far in the bomb-proof voices were heard saying: "Our old company commander has returned." "He that was wounded." "Kozeltsóf." "Michael Semyónitch," and so on; some even moved nearer to him, and the drummer greeted him.

"How do you do, Obantchoúk?" said Kozeltsóf. "Still whole? Good evening, lads'" he added, raising his voice.

The answer, "Wish your honour health!"resounded through the casemate.

"How are you getting on, lads?"

"Badly, your honour. The French are getting the better of us; they give it us hot from behind their 'trenchments, but don't come out into the open."

"Perhaps it will be my luck to see them coming out into the open, lads," said Kozeltsóf. "It won't be the first time for you and me, and we'll give them another thrashing."

"We'll do our best, your honour," several voices replied.

"There now, he's bold enough for anything!" said a voice.

"Awfully bold!" said the drummer to another soldier, not loud, but so as to be heard, and as if to justify the Commander's words, and to prove that there was nothing boastful or unlikely in what he had said.

From the soldiers Kozeltsóf went to join his fellow-officers in the Defensive Barracks.

XVI

A crowd of people were in the large barrack-room—naval, artillery, and infantry officers. Some slept, others talked, sitting on a chest of some kind and on the carriage of a garrison gun, but the largest and noisiest group sat on two Cossack cloaks spread on the floor beyond the arch, and were drinking porter and playing cards.

"Ah, Kozeltsóf! Kozeltsóf! . . . So you've come! That's good. . . . You're a brick. . . . How's your wound?" It was evident that here also he was liked, and his return gave pleasure.

When he had shaken hands with those he knew, Kozeltsóf joined the noisy group of officers playing cards. With some of them he was acquainted. A thin, dark, handsome man, with a long thin nose and large moustaches which grew out to his cheeks, kept the bank, and dealt the cards with thin, white fingers, on one of which he wore a large seal-ring with a crest. He dealt straight on and carelessly, being evidently excited about something, and only trying to appear at ease. At his right lay a grey-haired Major leaning on his elbows, who, with affected coolness, kept staking half-roubles and paying at once. On his left squatted an officer with a red, perspiring face, smiling unnaturally and joking. When his cards lost, he kept fumbling with one hand in his empty trouser-pocket. He was playing high, but evidently no longer for ready-money, and it was this that upset the handsome dark man. A bald, thin, pale officer with a huge nose and mouth paced the room with a large bundle of paper-money in his hand, and continually staked *va-banque* for ready money and won. Kozeltsóf drank a glass of *vódka* and sat down with the players.

"Stake something, Michael Semyónitch!" said the banker: "you've brought back lots of money, I'm sure."

"How should I get money! On the contrary, what I had I've spent in the town."

"Never! . . . You've surely cleared some one out in Simferópol!"

"I've really very little," said Kozeltsóf, but, evidently not wishing to be believed, he unbuttoned his uniform and took up an old pack of cards.

"Well, suppose I have a try; who knows what the devil may do for one! Even a mosquito, you know, wins his battles sometimes. Only I must have a drink to keep up my courage."

And soon, having drunk another glass of *vódka* and some porter, he lost his last three roubles.

A hundred and fifty roubles were noted down against the little perspiring officer.

"No, I've no luck," he said carelessly, preparing another card.

"I'll trouble you to send up the money," said the banker, ceasing for a moment to deal the cards and looking at him.

"Allow me to send it to-morrow," answered the perspiring officer, rising and fumbling with renewed vigour in his empty pocket.

"H'm!" bellowed the banker, and angrily throwing to the right and left, he finished the deal.

"But this won't do. I quit the bank. This won't do, Zahár Ivánitch," he repeated; "we are playing for ready money and not on credit."

"What! don't you trust me? It's really too ridiculous!"

"Who is going to pay me?" muttered the Major, who had won some eight roubles. "I have paid up more than twenty roubles and when I win I get nothing."

"How am I to pay," said the banker, "if there is no money on the board?"

"That's not my business," shouted the Major, rising; "I'm playing with you, and not with them."

The perspiring officer suddenly flared up:

"I shall pay to-morrow, I tell you. How dare you say such things to me?"

"I shall say what I please! That's no way to behave. There now!" shouted the Major.

"That's enough, Fyódor Fyódoritch!" said every one, restraining the Major.

But let us hasten to drop the curtain on this scene. To-morrow, or to-day, perhaps each of these men will cheerfully and proudly go to face death, and die steadfastly and calmly; but the only relief in these inhuman conditions, horrible even to the coldest imagination, and from which there is no hope of escape, is to forget and to destroy consciousness. Deep in each soul dwells a noble spark, capable of making him a hero; but the spark wearies of burning—a fateful moment may come when it will flash into flame and illuminate great deeds.

XVII

The next day the bombardment continued with equal vigour. At about eleven o'clock Volódya Kozeltsóf was sitting among the battery officers, to whom he was already beginning to get used. He was examining the new faces, observing, asking questions, and talking. The modest conversation, with a flavour of erudition, of the artillery officers inspired him with respect and pleased him. On the other hand, Volódya's bashful, innocent, and good-looking appearance inclined the officers in his favour. The senior of the battery, a Captain, a short man with reddish hair curling over his forehead and smoothed over the temples, brought up in the old artillery traditions, a ladies' man with a pretence to scientific knowledge, questioned Volódya about what he knew of artillery and of new inventions; joked in a friendly manner about his youth and his pretty face, and in general treated him as a son—and this Volódya liked very much. Sub-Lieutenant Dyádenko, a young officer who spoke with a Little-Russian accent, and had a torn cloak and dishevelled hair, though he talked loudly, snatched every opportunity to begin a cantankerous dispute, and was abrupt in his movements, nevertheless pleased Volódya, for he could not help seeing that a very kind heart, and much that was good, lay beneath this rough exterior. Dyádenko kept offering to be of use to Volódya, and demonstrating to him that none of the guns in Sevastopol were placed according to rule.

Lieutenant Tchernovítsky, with high-arched eyebrows, though he was the most polite of all, and his coat was clean enough and neatly patched if not very new, and though he showed a gold chain over his satin waistcoat, did not please Volódya. He kept asking what the Emperor and the Minister of War were doing, told him with unnatural rapture of feats of valour performed in Sevastopol, regretted there were so few real patriots, and in general displayed much knowledge, intelligence, and noble feeling; but, somehow, it all seemed unnatural and unpleasant to Volódya. He noticed especially that the other officers hardly spoke to Tchernovítsky. Junker Vlang, whom Volódya had disturbed the night before, was also there. He did not speak, but, sitting modestly in a corner, laughed when there was anything funny, helped to recall anything that was forgotten, handed the *vodka* bottle, and made cigarettes for all the officers. Whether it was the modest, courteous manner of Volódya, who behaved to him as to the officers and did not order him about as if he were a boy, or whether his attractive appearance charmed Vlánga (as the soldiers called him, giving a feminine form to his name), at any rate, he did not take his large, kind eyes from the new officer, foresaw and anticipated his wants, and was all the time in a state of enamoured ecstasy, which of course the officers noticed and made fun of.

Before dinner the Lieutenant-Captain was relieved from the bastion and joined them. Lieutenant-Captain Kraut was a fair-haired, handsome, and vivacious officer, with big, sandy moustaches and whiskers. He spoke Russian splendidly, but too accurately and elegantly for a Russian. In the service and in his life he was like his speech: he served admirably, was a first-rate comrade, most reliable in money matters; but simply as a man, just because everything was so satisfactory about him, something seemed lacking. Like all Russo-Germans, in strange contradistinction to the idealist German-Germans, he was *praktisch* in the extreme.

"Here he comes—our hero!" said the Captain, as Kraut came into the room swinging his arms and jingling his spurs. "What will you take, Friedrich Christiánitch, tea or *vódka?*"

"I have already ordered some tea," he answered, "but meanwhile I do not mind taking a drop of *vódka* as a refreshment to my soul.—Very pleased to make your acquaintance. I hope you will favour us with your company and your friendship," he said, turning to Volódya, who rose and bowed to him. "Lieutenant-Captain Kraut. . . . At the bastion yesterday, the master-gunner told me you had arrived."

"I am very grateful to you for your bed: I slept on it."

"But were you comfortable? One of the legs is broken: no one has time to mend it in this state of siege; it has to be propped up."

"Well, what luck have you had on duty?" asked Dyádenko.

"Oh, all right: only Skvortsóf was hit, and yesterday we had to mend a gun-carriage—the cheek was blown to shivers."

He rose and began to walk up and down. It was evident that he was under the influence of the pleasant feeling experienced by men who have just left a post of danger.

"Well, Dmitri Gavrílitch," he said, shaking the Captain by his knee, "how are you getting on? What of your recommendation—is it still silent?"

"There's no news as yet."

"And there won't be any," began Dyádenko: "I told you so before."

"Why won't there be?"

"Because the report was not written properly."

"Ah, you wrangler! you wrangler!" said Kraut, smiling merrily. "A real obstinate Little-Russian! There now, just to spite you, you'll be made Lieutenant."

"No, I shan't!"

"Vlang! get me my pipe and fill it," said Kraut, turning to the Junker, who rose at once and readily ran for the pipe.

Kraut brightened them all up: he talked of the bombardment, asked what had been going on in his absence, and spoke to every one.

XVIII

"Well, have you established yourself satisfactorily among us?" said Kraut to Volódya. "Pardon me! what is your name and patronymic? You know that's our custom in the artillery.... Have you a horse?"

"No," said Volódya; "I don't know what I am to do. I was telling the Captain . . . I have no horse, nor any money until I get my forage-money and travelling expenses paid. I thought, meanwhile, of asking the Commander of the battery to let me have a horse, but I'm afraid he will refuse."

"Apollon Sergéitch . . .?" and Kraut made a sound with his lips expressing strong doubt, and, looking at the Captain added, "hardly!"

"Well, if he does refuse there'll be no harm done," said the Captain. "To tell you the truth, a horse is not much wanted here; still, it is worth trying. I will ask him to-day."

"How little you know him," Dyádenko put in: "he might refuse anything else, but not that.... Will you bet?"

"Well, of course we know you can't help contradicting."

"I contradict because I know: he's close in other matters, but he'll give a horse because he gains nothing by refusing."

"Gains nothing when oats are eight roubles? "said Kraut: "the gain is not having to keep an extra horse!"

"You ask for Skvoréts, Vladimir Semyónitch," said Vlang, returning with Kraut's pipe: "it's a capital horse."

"Off which you fell into a ditch in Soróki, eh, Vlánga?" remarked the Lieutenant-Captain.

"What does it matter if oats are eight roubles when, in his estimates, they figure at ten and a half?[52] That's where the gain comes in," said Dyádenko, continuing to argue.

"Well, naturally, you can't expect him to keep nothing. When you are commander of a battery, I dare say you'll not let one have a horse to ride into town."

---

[52] Referring to the custom of charging the Government more than the actual price of supplies, and thereby making an income which was supposed to go for the benefit of the regiment, but part of which frequently remained unaccounted for.

"When I am the commander of a battery, my horses will get four measures each, and I shall not make an income, no fear!"

"We shall see, if we live . . ." said the Lieutenant-Captain: "you will act in just the same way—and so will he," pointing to Volódya.

"Why do you think that he too would wish to make a profit," said Tchernovítsky to Kraut: "he may have private means, then why should he make a profit?"

"Oh no, I . . . excuse me, Captain," said Volódya, blushing up to his ears, "but I should think such a thing dishonourable."

"Dear me! what a severe fellow he is!" said Kraut.

"No, I only mean that I think that if the money is not mine, I ought not to take it."

"But I'll just tell you something, young man," began the Lieutenant-Captain, in a more serious tone; "do you know that if you are commanding a battery you have to conduct things properly, and that's enough. The commander of a battery does not interfere with the soldiers' supplies; that's always been the custom in the artillery. If you are a bad manager, you will have no surplus. But you have to spend over and above what's in the estimates: for shoeing—that's one" (he bent down one finger), "and for medicine—that's two" (and he bent down another finger), "for office expenses—that's three: then for off-horses one has to pay up to 500 roubles, my dear fellow—that's four: you have to supply the soldiers with new collars, spend a good bit on charcoal for the *samovárs*, and keep open table for the officers. If you are in command of a battery you must live decently: you must have a carriage and a fur coat, and one thing and another. . . . It's quite plain!"

"And above all," interrupted the Captain, who had been silent all the time, "look here, Vladimir Semyón-itch. Imagine a man, like myself say, serving for twenty years, with a pay of first 200, then 300 roubles a year. Can one refuse him a crust of bread in his old age, after all his service?"

"Ah, what's the good of talking," again began the Lieutenant-Captain: "don't be in a hurry to judge, but live and serve."

Volódya felt horribly confused and ashamed of what he had so thoughtlessly said; he muttered something, and then listened in silence while Dyádenko began, very irritably, disputing and proving the contrary of what had been said. The dispute was interrupted by the Colonel's orderly, who came to say that dinner was served.

"Ask Apollón Sergéitch to give us some wine today," said Tchernovítsky to the Captain, buttoning his uniform. "Why is he so stingy? If we get killed it will all be wasted."

"Well, ask him yourself."

"Oh no; you are the senior officer: we must observe order in all things."

XIX

The table had been moved away from the wall and covered with a dirty tablecloth in the room where Volódya had presented himself to the Colonel the night before. To-day the Commander of the battery shook hands with him, and asked him the Petersburg news and about his journey.

"Well, gentlemen, who takes *vódka?* Please help yourselves—ensigns don't take any," added he with a smile.

Altogether he did not seem at all as stern as the night before: on the contrary, he seemed a kind and hospitable host, and an elder comrade among his fellow-officers. But, in spite of it all, the officers, from the old Captain down to Ensign Dyádenko, showed him great respect, if only by the way they addressed him, politely looking him straight in the eyes, and by the timid way they came up, one by one, to the side-table to drink their glass of *vódka.*

The dinner consisted of a large tureen of cabbage-soup seasoned with an enormous quantity of pepper and bay-leaves, and in which floated pieces of fat beef; Polish cutlets with mustard, and dumplings with butter that was not very fresh. There were no napkins, the spoons were pewter and wooden; there were only two tumblers, and on the table the only drink was supplied by a water-bottle with a broken neck; but the meal was not dull: the conversation never flagged. At first they talked about the battle of Inkerman, in which the battery had taken part, and each gave his own impressions of it and reasons for the reverse, but all were silent as soon as the Commander spoke. Then the conversation naturally passed on to the insufficient calibre of the field-guns, and to the subject of new lighter cannons, which gave Volódya an opportunity of showing his knowledge of artillery. But the conversation never touched the present terrible condition of Sevastopol: it was as if each one had thought so much on this subject that he did not wish to speak of it. Nor, to Volódya's great surprise and regret, was there any mention at all of the duties of the service on which he had entered; it was as if he had come to Sevastopol solely to discuss lighter guns and to dine with the Commander of the battery. During the dinner a bomb fell near the house they were in. The floor and walls vibrated as if from an earthquake, and the windows were darkened by powder smoke.

"You didn't see that sort of thing in Petersburg, I fancy; but here we get many such surprises," said the Commander of the battery. "Vlang, go and see where it burst."

Vlang went out to see, and reported that it had fallen in the square; and no more was said about the bomb.

Just before dinner ended, a little old man, the battery-clerk, came into the room with three sealed envelopes and handed them to the Commander: "This one is very important: a Cossack has just brought it from the Chief of the Artillery."

All the officers looked with eager impatience as the Commander, with practised fingers, broke the seal, and drew out the *very important* paper. "What can it be?" each one asked himself. It might be an order to retire from Sevastopol to recuperate, or the whole battery might be ordered to the bastions.

"Again!" said the Commander, angrily throwing the paper on the table.

"What is it, Apollón Sergéitch?" asked the senior officer.

"They order an officer and men to some mortar-battery or other. . . . As it is, I have only four officers and not men enough for the gun detachments," grumbled the Commander of the battery; "and here they are taking more away. . . . However, gentlemen, some one will have to go," said he after a short silence: "the order is, to be at the outposts at seven. Send the Sergeant-major to me. Well, who will go? Decide, gentlemen."

"There,—he has not been anywhere yet," said Tchernovítsky, pointing to Volódya.

The Commander of the battery did not answer.

"Yes, I should like to go," said Volódya, and he felt the cold sweat break out on his back and neck.

"No, why? "interrupted the Captain. "Of course no one would refuse, but one need not offer oneself either: but if Apollón Sergéitch leaves it to us, let us throw lots, as we did last time."

All agreed. Kraut cut up some paper, rolled up the bits, and threw them into a cap. The Captain joked, and even ventured, on this occasion, to ask the Colonel for some wine—to keep up their courage, as he said. Dyádenko sat looking grim, Volódya smiled at something. Tchernovítsky declared he was sure to draw it. Kraut was perfectly calm. Volódya was allowed to draw first. He took a roll of paper a bit longer than the others, but then decided to change it; and taking a thinner and shorter one, unrolled it and read "Go."

"It's I," he said with a sigh.

"Well, God be with you; you'll get your baptism of fire at once," said the Commander, looking at. the Ensign's perturbed face with a kindly smile "but make haste and get ready, and so that it shall be pleasanter for you, Vlang shall go with you as gun-sergeant."

XX

Vlang was extremely pleased with his appointment, ran off quickly to get ready, and when dressed came to help Volódya: trying to persuade him to take a bed, a fur coat, some back numbers of *Fatherland Records*, the coffee-pot with the spirit lamp, and other unnecessary things. The Captain advised Volódya to read up in the Handbook (Bezák's *Artillery Officer's Handbook*) about firing mortars, and especially to copy out the tables in it. Volódya set to work at once, and to his surprise and joy noticed that his fear of the danger, and, more still, of being a coward, though it still troubled him a little, was far from what it had been the night before. This was partly the effect of daylight and activity, but was chiefly due to the fact that fear, like every strong feeling, cannot long continue with the same intensity. In short, he had already had time to live through the worst of it. At about seven o'clock, just as the sun began to disappear behind the Nicholas Barracks, the Sergeant-major came and announced that the men were ready and waiting.

"I have given Vlánga the list; your honour will please receive it from him," said he.

About twenty artillerymen, with only their side-arms, stood behind the corner of the house. Volódya and the Junker walked up to them. "Shall I make them a little speech, or simply say 'Good-day, lads,' or say nothing at all," he thought. "But why not say 'Good-day, lads;' it is even right that I should," and he cried boldly with his ringing voice, "Good-day, lads!" The soldiers answered gaily: the young, fresh voice sounded pleasantly in the ears of each. Volódya went briskly in front of the soldiers, and though his heart beat as fast as if he had run full-speed for miles, his step was light and his face cheerful. When they were approaching the Maláhof Redoubt, mounting the hill, he noticed that Vlang, who kept close to him all the time, and who had seemed so brave before leaving the house, was continually dodging and stooping, as if all the bombs and cannon-balls, which here whistled past very frequently, were flying straight at him. Some of the soldiers did the same, and, in general, most of the faces expressed uneasiness, if not exactly alarm. These circumstances completely comforted and emboldened Volódya.

"So here I, also, am on the Maláhof mound, which I fancied a thousand times more terrible. And I get along without bowing to the balls, and am even much less frightened than the others. So I am no coward," thought he, with pleasure and even a certain rapturous self-complacency.

This feeling, however, was quickly shaken by a sight he came upon in the twilight on the Kornílof Battery while looking for the Commander of the bastion. Four sailors stood by the breastwork holding by its arms and legs the bloody corpse of a man without boots or coat, swinging it before heaving it over. (On the second day of this bombardment it was found impossible in some parts to clear away the corpses from the bastions, and they were, therefore, thrown out into the ditch, so as not to be in the way at the batteries.) Volódya felt stunned for a moment when he saw the body bump on the top of the breastwork and then roll down into the ditch, but, luckily for him, the Commander of the bastion met him just then and gave him his orders, as well as a guide to show him the way to the battery and to the bomb-proof assigned to his men. We will not speak of all the dangers and disenchantments our hero lived through that evening; how—instead of the firing he was used to on the Vólkof field, amid conditions of perfect exactitude and order, which he had expected to meet with here also,—he found two injured mortars, one with its mouth battered in by a ball, the other standing on the splinters of its shattered platform; how he could not get workmen to mend the platform till the morning; how not a single charge was of the weight specified in the Handbook; how two of the men under him were wounded, and how he was twenty times within a hair's-breadth of death. Fortunately a gigantic gunner, a seaman who had served with the mortars since the commencement of the siege, had been appointed to assist Volódya, and convinced him of the possibility of using the mortars. By the light of a lantern, this gunner showed him all over the battery as he might have shown him over his own kitchen-garden, and undertook to have everything right by the morning. The bomb-proof to which his guide led him was an oblong hole dug in the rocky ground, 25 cubic yards in size and covered with oak beams nearly 2½ feet thick. He and all his soldiers installed themselves in it.

Vlang first of all, as soon as he discovered the little door, not a yard high, rushed in headlong at the risk of breaking his limbs against the stone bottom, squeezed into the farthest corner and there remained. Volódya, when all the soldiers had settled on the ground along the walls, and some had lit their pipes, made up his bed in a corner, lit a candle, and, after lighting a cigarette, lay down.

The reports of the continuous firing could be heard overhead, but not very distinctly, except from one cannon which stood quite close and shook the bombproof with its thunder. In the bomb-proof all was quiet, except when one or other of the soldiers, still rather shy in the presence of the new officer, spoke, asking a neighbour to move a little, or to give him a light for his pipe, when a rat scratched somewhere among the stones, or when Vlang, who had not yet recovered, and was still looking wildly around him, heaved a deep sigh.

Volódya, on his bed in this quiet corner crammed with people and lighted by a solitary candle, experienced a sensation of cosiness such as he had felt as a child when, playing hide-and-seek, he used to creep into the cupboard or under his mother's skirt and sit listening in breathless silence, afraid of the dark, yet conscious of enjoyment. It felt rather uncanny, yet his spirits were high.

After ten minutes or so the soldiers grew bolder and began to talk. The more important people—two noncommissioned officers, an old grey-haired one with all the medals and crosses except that of St. George, and a young one, a Cantonist,[53] who was smoking cigarettes made by himself—had settled nearest to the light and to the officer's bed. The drummer had, as usual, taken upon himself the duty of waiting upon the officer. The bombardiers and men who had medals came next, and farther on, in the shadow nearer the entrance, sat the meeker folk. It was these last who started the conversation.

---

[53] The Cantonists, in the old days of serfdom, were the sons of soldiers, condemned by law and heredity to be soldiers also.

The cause of it was the noise made by a man who came tumbling hastily into the bomb-proof.

"Hullo, old fellow! how's it you don't stay outside? Don't the lasses play merrily enough out there?" said a voice.

"They're playing such tunes as we never hear in our village," laughingly answered the man who had just run in.

"Ah! Vásin don't like bombs—ah! he don't," said some one in the aristocratic corner.

"If there were any need it would be quite a different thing," slowly replied Vásin; and when he spoke all the others were silent "On the 24th at least we were working the guns; but what's there to find fault with now? If we get killed uselessly the authorities won't thank the likes of us for it."

At these words all laughed.

"There's Mélnikof—he's out there now, I fancy," said some one.

"Go and send that Mélnikof in here," said the old sergeant, "or else he'll really get killed uselessly."

"Who is Mélnikof?" asked Volódya.

"Oh, it's a poor, silly soldier of ours, your honour. He's just afraid of nothing, and he's now walking about outside. You should have a look at him; he's just like a bear."

"He knows a charm," came Vásin's long-drawn accents from the other corner.

Mélnikof entered the bomb-proof. He was stout (which is extremely rare among soldiers), red-haired and red-faced, and had an enormous bulging forehead and prominent, clear, blue eyes.

"Aren't you afraid of the bombs?" asked Volódya.

"What's there to be afraid of in them bombs?" answered Mélnikof, shrugging and scratching himself; "they'll not kill me with a bomb, I know."

"So you would like to live here?"

"In course I should. It's gay here," he said, and burst out laughing.

"Oh, then they should take you for a sortie! Shall I speak to the General about it?" said Volódya, though he did not know a single General here.

"Like, indeed! In course I should!" And Mélnikof hid behind the others.

"Let's have a game of 'noses,' lads! Who has got cards?" his voice was heard to say hurriedly.

And soon the game had started in the far corner: one could hear laughter, noses being smacked, and trumps declared. Volódya drank some tea—the drummer having heated the *samovár* for him—treated the non-commissioned officers to some, joked and talked with them, wishing to gain popularity, and felt very pleased at the respect paid him. The soldiers also, seeing that the gentleman gave himself no airs, became talkative. One of them explained that the siege of Sevastopol would not last much longer, because a reliable fellow in the fleet had told him that Constantine, the Tsar's brother, was coming with the 'Merican fleet to help us; and also that there would soon be an agreement not to fire for a fortnight, but to have a rest, and that if any one did fire he'd have to pay a fine of seventy-five kopéykas for each shot. Vásin, who, as Volódya had already observed, was small, and had whiskers and kind, large eyes, related, first amid general silence and then amid roars of laughter, how he had gone home on leave, and at first every one was glad to see him; but then his father began sending him to work, and the Forester-Lieutenant sent a horse and trap to fetch his wife! All this amused Volódya very much. He not only felt no fear, or discomfort from the overcrowding and bad air in the bomb-proof, but, on the contrary, felt exceedingly bright and contented.

Many of the soldiers were already snoring. Vlang also lay stretched on the floor, and the old sergeant, having spread his cloak on the ground, was crossing himself and muttering prayers before going to sleep, when Volódya felt inclined to go out of the bombproof and see what was going on outside.

"Draw in your legs!" the soldiers called to one another as soon as he rose, and the legs, drawing in, made room for him.

Vlang, who had seemed to be asleep, suddenly raised his head and seized Volódya by the skirts of his cloak.

"Now don't; don't go—how can you?" he began in a tearfully persuasive voice. "You do not yet know; out there the cannon-balls fall without stopping. It's better in here."

But in spite of Vlang's entreaties, Volódya made his way out of the bomb-proof and sat down on the threshold, where Mélnikof was already sitting.

The air was pure and fresh, especially compared with that in the bomb-proof; the night was clear and calm. Amid the booming of the cannons one could hear the wheels of carts bringing gabions, and the voices of men at work in the powder-vault. High overhead was the starry sky, across which ran the fiery trails of the bombs. To the left was another bomb-proof, through the small entrance to which the legs and backs of the sailors who lived there could be discerned and their voices heard. In front was the roof of the powder-vault, past which flitted the figures of stooping men, while on it a tall form in a black cloak stood, with his hands in his pockets, under the bullets and bombs that incessantly flew past the spot, and kept treading down with his heel the earth that other men brought there in sacks. Many a bomb flew past and exploded near the vault The soldiers who were carrying the earth stooped and stepped aside; but the black figure continued calmly to stamp the earth down with his feet, and remained on the spot in the same position.

"Who is that black fellow there?" said Volódya to Mélnikof.

"Can't say. I'll go and see."

"No, don't; there's no need."

But Mélnikof rose without heeding him, approached the black figure and for a long time stood by it equally indifferent and immovable.

"That's the powder-master, your honour!" he said when he returned. "The vault has been knocked in by a bomb, so the infantry men are carrying earth there."

Now and then a bomb seemed to fly straight at the door of the bomb-proof. Then Volódya pressed behind the corner, but soon crept out again, looking up to see if another was coming that way. Though Vlang, from inside the bomb-proof, again and again entreated him to come in, Volódya sat at the threshold for about three hours, finding a kind of pleasure in tempting fate and in watching the flying bombs. By the end of the evening he knew how many guns were firing, from which positions, and where their shots fell.

XXII

The next morning, the 27th of August, Volódya, after several hours' sleep, came out fresh and vigorous to the threshold of the bomb-proof. Vlang also came out, but at the first sound of a bullet he rushed wildly back through the entrance, pushing his way through the crowd with his head, amid the general laughter of the soldiers, most of whom had also come out into the fresh air.

Vlang, the old sergeant, and a few others, only came out into the trench at rare intervals, but the rest could not be kept inside: they all crept out of the stuffy bomb-proof into the fresh morning air, and in spite of the firing, which continued as violently as on the day before, they settled themselves—some by the threshold of the bomb-proof, and some under the breastwork. Mélnikof had been strolling about from battery to battery since early dawn, looking calmly upwards.

Near the threshold sat two old [soldiers and one young, curly-haired one, a Jew transferred to the battery from an infantry regiment. This soldier had picked up one of the bullets that were lying about, and after flattening it out on a stone with the fragment of a bomb, was now carving out a cross like the Order of St. George; the others sat talking and watching his work. The cross was really turning out very handsome.

"I say," said one of them, "if we remain here much longer, then, when there's peace, we shall all have served our time and get discharged."

"Sure enough! Why, I had only four years left to serve, and here I am five months at Sevastopol."

"That's not counted specially to the discharge, you know," said another.

At this moment a cannon-ball flew over the heads of the speakers and fell a couple of feet from Mélnikof, who was approaching them through the trench.

"It nearly killed Mélnikof," said one of them.

"It won't kill me," said Mélnikof.

"Then here you have a cross for your courage," said the young soldier, giving him the cross he had made.

"... No, my lad; a month's service here counts as a year for everything—that was said in the order," continued one of the soldiers.

"You may say what you like, but when we've peace we're sure to have an Imperial review at Warsaw, and then, if we don't all get our discharge we shall be put on the permanent reserve."

Just then a shrieking, glancing rifle-ball flew just over the talkers' heads and struck a stone.

"Mind, or you'll get your discharge in full before to-night," said one of the soldiers.

They all laughed.

And not only before night, but before two hours had passed, two of them had got their discharge in full, and five more were wounded; but the rest went on joking just the same.

By the morning, sure enough, the two mortars had really been put into such condition that it was possible to fire them. At ten o'clock Volódya, in accordance with the order he had received from the chief of the bastion, called out his company and marched with it to the battery.

Among the men not a trace of the fear which had been noticeable the day before remained as soon as they were actively engaged. Only Vlang could not master himself, but hid and ducked in the same old way, and Vásin lost some of his composure and fidgetted and kept dodging. Volódya was in ecstasies; the thought of danger never entered his head. Joy at fulfilling his duty, at finding that he was not only no coward, but was even brave; the sense of commanding and being in the presence of twenty men who were, he knew, watching him with curiosity, made him quite valiant. He was even vain of his courage, and showed off before the soldiers; climbed out on to the banquette, and unfastened his cloak on purpose to be more conspicuous. The Commander of the bastion, making the round of his 'household,' as he expressed it, used as he had become in the last eight months to courage of all sorts, could not help admiring this pretty boy, his unbuttoned cloak showing a red shirt closing round his delicate white neck, as with flushed face and glistening eyes he clapped his hands and gave, in ringing tones, the order, "One—two!" and ran lightly on to the breastwork to see where his bombs were falling. At half-past eleven the firing slackened on both sides, and just at twelve commenced the storming of the Maláhof Redoubt, and of the Second, Third (the Redan), and Fifth Bastions.

XXIII

On the North Side of the Roadstead, at the Star Fort, near noon, two seamen stood on the 'telegraph' mound; one of them, an officer, was looking at Sevastopol through the fixed telescope. Another officer, accompanied by a Cossack, had just ridden up to join him at the big Signal-post

The sun stood high and bright above the Roadstead, which, in the glad, warm light, was playing with its ships at anchor, with their sails and with the boats. The light breeze softly rustled among the dying leaves of the oak bushes near the 'telegraph,' filled the sails of the boats and rocked the waves. Sevastopol—still the same: with its unfinished church, its column, its quay, its green boulevard on the hill, its elegant library building, its azure creeks filled with masts, its picturesque aqueduct arches, and with blue clouds of powder-smoke now and then lit up by the blood-red flame of a cannon; the same beautiful, gay, proud Sevastopol, bounded on the one side by the yellow, smoking hills, on the other by the bright blue water of the sea, glittering in the sunlight—lay on the other side of the Roadstead. Above the sea-line, along which the smoke of some passing steamer left a black trail, floated long white clouds which promised wind.

Along the whole line of fortifications, but especially on the high ground on the left side, appeared, several at a time, with lightnings that at times flashed bright even in the noonday sun, puffs of thick, dense, white smoke, that grew, taking various shapes, and appearing darker against the sky. These clouds, showing now here, now there, appeared on the hills, on the enemy's batteries, in the town, and high up in the sky. The reports of explosions never ceased, but rolled together and rent the air.

Towards noon the puffs appeared more and more rarely, and the air vibrated less with the booming.

"I say, the Second Bastion does not reply at all now!" said the hussar officer on horseback; "it is quite knocked to pieces. Terrible!"

"Yes, and the Maláhof, too, sends hardly one shot in reply to three of theirs," said he who was looking through the telescope. "Their silence provokes me! They are shooting straight into the Kornílof Battery, and it does not reply."

"But look there! I told you that they always cease the bombardment about noon. It's the same today. Come, let's go to lunch; they'll be waiting for us already. What's the good of looking?"

"Don't! wait a bit!" answered the one who had possession of the telescope, looking very eagerly towards Sevastopol.

"What is it? What?"

"A movement in the entrenchments, thick columns advancing."

"Yes! They can be seen even without a glass, marching in columns. The alarm must be given," said the seaman.

"Look! look! They've left the trenches!"

And, really, with the naked eye one could see what looked like dark spots moving down the hill from the French batteries across the valley to the bastions. In front of these spots dark stripes were already visibly approaching our line. On the bastions white cloudlets burst in succession as if chasing one another. The wind brought a sound of rapid small-arm firing like the beating of rain against a window. The dark stripes were moving in the midst of the smoke and came nearer and nearer. The sounds of firing, growing stronger and stronger, mingled in a prolonged, rumbling peal. Puffs of smoke rose more and more often, spread rapidly along the line, and at last formed one lilac cloud (dotted here and there with little faint lights and black spots), which kept curling and uncurling; and all the sounds blended into one tremendous clatter.

"An assault!" said the naval officer, turning pale and letting the seaman look through the telescope.

Cossacks galloped along the road, some officers rode by, the Commander-in-Chief passed in a carriage with his suite. Every face showed painful excitement and expectation.

"It's impossible they can have taken it," said the mounted officer.

"By God, a standard! . . . Look! look!" said the other, panting, and walked away from the telescope: "A French standard on the Maláhof!"

"It can't be!"

XXIV

The elder Koseltsóf, who had during the preceding night won back his money and then again before morning lost everything, including the gold pieces sewn in his cuff, was lying in a heavy, unhealthy, but sound sleep in the Defensive Barracks of the Fifth Bastion, when a fateful cry arose, repeated by many voices—

"The alarm!"

"Why are you sleeping, Michael Semyónitch! We are attacked!" shouted some one.

"It must be a hoax," he said, opening his eyes incredulously.

But suddenly he saw an officer running, without any apparent object, from one corner of the barrack to the other with such a pale face that he understood it all. The thought that they might take him for a coward who did not wish to be with his company at a critical moment upset him terribly. He rushed as fast as he could to join it The artillery firing had ceased, but the clatter of musketry was at its height. The bullets did not whistle as single ones do, but came in swarms like a flock of autumn birds flying overhead.

The whole place where his battalion was stationed the day before was hidden in smoke, and angry shouts and exclamations were heard. Crowds of soldiers, wounded and not wounded, met him as he went. Having run another thirty paces he saw his company pressing to the wall.

"The Schwartz Redoubt is taken!" said a young officer. "All is lost!"

"Nonsense!" he said angrily, and drawing his little blunt iron sword, he cried—

"Forward, lads! Hurrah!"

His own loud, clear voice roused Koseltsóf himself. He ran forward along the traverse, and about fifty soldiers ran shouting after him. From the traverse he ran out into the open ground. The bullets fell just like hailstones. Two hit him, but where, and what they had done—bruised or wounded him—he had no time to determine. Before him, through the smoke, he could already see blue uniforms and red trousers and could hear cries that were not Russian. One Frenchman stood on the breastwork waving his cap and shouting something. Kozeltsóf felt sure he would be killed, and this increased his courage. He ran on and on. Several soldiers outran him, others appeared from somewhere else and also ran. The blue uniforms remained at the same distance from him, running back to their trenches, but there were dead and wounded on the ground under his feet. When he had run to the outer ditch all became blurred to Kozeltsóf's eyes, and he felt a pain in his chest.

Half-an-hour later he was lying on a stretcher by the Nicholas Barracks, and he knew that he was wounded, but felt hardly any pain. He only wished for something cool to drink and to lie more comfortably.

A little, plump doctor with large black whiskers came up to him and unbuttoned his cloak. Kozeltsóf looked over his chin to see what the doctor was doing to his wound, and at the doctor's face, but he still felt no pain. The doctor covered the wound with the shirt, wiped his fingers on the skirt of his cloak, and silently, without looking at the wounded man, passed on to another patient. Kozeltsóf watched unconsciously what was going on around him, and remembering what had happened at the Fifth Bastion with an exceedingly joyful feeling of self-satisfaction, thought that he had performed his duty well,—that for the first time during his whole service, he had acted as well as was possible and had nothing to reproach himself with. The doctor, bandaging another man, pointed to Kozeltsóf and said something to a priest with a large red beard who stood nearby with a cross.

"Am I dying?" asked Kozeltsóf, when the priest approached him.

The priest, without replying, said a prayer and held the cross to the lips of the wounded man.

Death did not frighten Kozeltsóf. He took the cross with his weak hands, pressed it to his lips and began to weep.

"Were the French driven back?" he asked the priest

"The victory is ours at all points," answered the latter to console the wounded man, hiding from him the fact that from the Maláhof Redoubt the French standard was already waving.

"Thank God!" exclaimed the dying man. He did not feel the tears that ran down his cheeks.

The thought of his brother flashed through his brain:

"God grant him as good a fate," thought he.

XXV

But a different fate awaited Volódya. He was listening to a tale Vásin was telling when he heard the cry, "The French are coming!" The blood rushed suddenly to his heart, and he felt his cheeks grow cold and pale. He remained immovable for a moment, but glancing round, he saw the soldiers pretty coolly fastening their uniforms and crawling out one after the other. One of them—Mélnikof probably—even joked, saying," Let's meet them with bread and salt."[54]

Volódya and Vlang, who followed him like his shadow, climbed out of the bomb-proof and ran to the battery. There was no artillery firing at all on either side. The quiet appearance of the soldiers did less to rouse Volódya than the pitiful cowardice of the

---

[54] It is a Russian custom to offer bread and salt to new arrivals.

Junker. "Can I possibly be like him?" he thought, and ran gaily up to the breastwork where his mortars stood. He could plainly see the French running straight towards him across the open ground, and crowds of them moving in the nearer trenches, their bayonets glittering in the sunshine. One short, broad-shouldered fellow in a Zouave uniform ran in front, sword in hand, jumping across the pits.

"Fire with case-shot!" cried Volódya, running down from the banquette; but the soldiers had made their arrangements without waiting for his orders, and the metallic ring of the escaping case-shot whistled over his head, first from one mortar and then from the other. "One—Two!" ordered Volódya, running the distance between the two mortars and quite forgetting the danger. From one side, and near at hand, the clatter of the muskets of our supports mingled with excited cries.

Suddenly a wild cry of despair arose on the left. "They're behind us! behind us!" was repeated by several voices. Volódya looked round. About twenty Frenchmen appeared behind him. One of them, a handsome man with a black beard, was ahead of the rest, but when he had run up to within ten paces of the battery he stopped, fired point-blank at Volódya, and then again started running towards him. For a moment Volódya stood petrified, unable to believe his eyes. When he recollected himself and glanced round, he saw French uniforms on the breastwork in front of him; two Frenchmen, about ten paces from him, were even spiking a cannon. No one was near but Mélnikof, who had fallen at his side killed by a bullet, and Vlang, who had seized a linstock and was rushing forward with a furious look on his face, rolling his eyes and shouting. "Follow me, Vladimir Semyónitch! . . . Follow me!" cried Vlang in a desperate voice, brandishing his linstock at the Frenchmen who had come up from behind. The ferocious figure of the Junker perplexed them. Vlang hit the front one on the head; the others involuntarily hesitated, and continually looking back and shouting desperately, "Follow me, Vladimir Semyónitch; why are you stopping? run!" he ran to the trench where our infantry lay firing at the French. Having jumped in, he climbed out again to see what his adored Ensign was doing. Something in a cloak lay prostrate where Volódya had stood, and the whole of that part was covered with Frenchmen firing at our men.

XXVI

Vlang found his company at the second line of defence. Of the twenty soldiers who had gone to the mortar battery, only eight had escaped.

Towards nine in the evening Vlang with the battery crossed over to the North Side on a steamer filled with soldiers, cannon, horses, and wounded men. There was no firing anywhere. The stars shone as brightly in the sky as they had done the night before, but a strong wind rocked the waves. On the First and Second Bastions flames kept bursting up along the ground; explosions rent the air and lit up around them strange dark objects and stones flying in the air. Something was burning near the docks, and the red glare was reflected in the water. The bridge, thronged with people, was illuminated by the fire on the Nicholas Battery. A large flame seemed to stand above the water on the distant little headland of the Alexander Battery, lighting up from below the clouds of smoke that hung above it; and quiet, insolent, distant lights gleamed over the sea, as they had done yesterday, from the fleet of the enemy. A fresh wind rocked the Roadstead. By the glaring light of the conflagrations one could see the masts of our sinking ships, which were slowly descending deeper and deeper into the water. No one was talking on board only the words of command given by the captain, the snorting and stamping of the animals on the vessel, and the moaning of the wounded, were heard above the steam and the regular swish of the parting waters. Vlang, who had not eaten all day, took a piece of bread from his pocket and began munching it; but suddenly remembering Volódya, he began to cry so loud that the soldiers near him heard it.

"Look! he has bread to eat, and still he cries, our Vlánga does!" said Vásin.

"That's queer," said another. "Look! our barrack has been fired as well," continued he with a sigh; "and how many of the likes of us have perished; and the Frenchmen have got it for nothing."

"At all events, we have got off alive, thank heaven!" said Vásin.

"It's a shame, for all that."

"Where's the shame? D'you think they'll get a chance of amusing themselves out there? See if ours don't take it back. Never mind how many of the likes of us is lost; if the Emperor gives the word, as sure as there's a God we'll take it back. You don't suppose ours will just leave it so? No fear! Here you are; take the bare walls . . . The 'trenchments are all blown up . . . Yes, I daresay . . . *He's* stuck his flag on the mound, but he's not gone and shoved himself into the town. You wait a bit! The real reckoning will come—only wait a bit," he concluded, admonishing the French.

"Of course it will!" said another with conviction.

Along the whole line of the Sevastopol bastions, which for so many months had been seething with such amazingly energetic life, for so many months had seen heroes relieved by death as they fell one after another, and for so many months had aroused the fear, the hatred, and at last the admiration of the enemy—on these bastions no one was now to be seen. All was dead, ghastly, terrible, but not silent: the destruction still went on. Everywhere on the earth, blasted and strewn around by fresh explosions, lay shattered gun-carriages, crushing the corpses of foes and Russians alike; cast-iron cannons, silenced for ever, thrown with terrific force into holes and half-buried in the earth; bombs, cannon-balls and more dead bodies, then holes and splintered beams from the bomb-proofs, and again silent corpses in grey and blue uniforms. All this still shuddered again and again, and was lit up by the lurid flames of the explosions that continued to shake the air.

The enemy saw that something incomprehensible was happening in awe-inspiring Sevastopol. The explosions and the deathly stillness on the bastions made them shudder; but still, under the influence of the strong and firm resistance of that day, they dared not yet believe that their unflinching foe had vanished; and silently, and anxiously immovable, they awaited the end of the sombre night

The Sevastopol army, surging and spreading like the sea on a rough, dark night, anxiously palpitating through all its members, moved through the dense darkness, slowly swaying, by the bridge over the Roadstead, and on to the North Side, away from the place where it was leaving so many brave brothers, from the place saturated with its blood, from the place which it had held for eleven months from a far stronger foe, but which it was now commanded to abandon without a struggle.

The first effect this command had on every Russian was one of oppressive bewilderment. The next sensation was fear of pursuit The men felt helpless as soon as they had left the places where they were accustomed to fight, and they crowded anxiously together in the darkness at the entrance to the bridge, which was rocked by the strong wind. With bayonets clashing one against another—line regiments, ships' crews, and militiamen jumbled together—those on foot pressed onward, mounted officers bearing orders forced their way, inhabitants and orderlies with loads, which were not allowed to pass, wept and implored, while the artillery with noisy wheels, hurrying to get away, moved towards the bay. Notwithstanding the diversion resulting from their various and varied occupations, the instinct of self-preservation and the desire to get away from this dreadful place of death as quickly as possible was present in the soul of each. It was present in the mortally wounded soldier who lay, among 500 other wounded men, on the pavement of the Pávlof Quay, praying to God for death; and in the militiaman pushing with all his might into the dense crowd to make way for a general who rode past; and in the general who conducted the crossing, firmly restraining the impetuosity of the soldiers; and in the sailor who, having got among the moving battalions, was squeezed by the swaying crowd till he could scarcely breathe; and in the wounded officer whom four soldiers had been carrying on a stretcher, but whom, stopped by the throng, they had been obliged to lay on the ground near the Nicholas Battery; and in the artilleryman who, having served for sixteen years with the same gun, now, in obedience to an officer's orders, quite incomprehensible to him, was, with the aid of his comrades, pushing that gun down the steep bank into the Roadstead; and in the sailors of the fleet who, having just knocked out the scuttles in the ships, were briskly rowing away from them in their long-boats. On reaching the North Side and leaving the bridge, almost every man took off his cap and crossed himself. But behind this feeling there was another, a sad, gnawing, and deeper feeling, which seemed like remorse, shame, and anger. Almost every soldier, looking back from the North Side at the abandoned town, sighed with inexpressible bitterness in his heart, and menaced the enemy.

THE END

CPSIA information can be obtained
at www.ICGtesting.com
Printed in the USA
LVHW03s1849230718
584651LV00002B/318/P

9 781420 949285